Palgrave Science Fiction and Fantasy: A New Canon

Series Editors
Anna McFarlane
Medical Humanities Research Group
University of Leeds
Dundee, UK

Timothy S. Miller
Boca Raton, USA

Palgrave Science Fiction and Fantasy: A New Canon provides short introductions to key works of science fiction and fantasy (SFF) speaking to why a text, trilogy, or series matters to SFF as a genre as well as to readers, scholars, and fans. These books aim to serve as a go-to resource for thinking on specific texts and series and for prompting further inquiry. Each book will be less than 30,000 words and structured similarly to facilitate classroom use. Focusing specifically on literature, the books will also address film and TV adaptations of the texts as relevant. Beginning with background and context on the text's place in the field, the author and how this text fits in their oeuvre, and the socio-historical reception of the text, the books will provide an understanding of how students, readers, and scholars can think dynamically about a given text. Each book will describe the major approaches to the text and how the critical engagements with the text have shaped SFF. Engaging with classic works as well as recent books that have been taken up by SFF fans and scholars, the goal of the series is not to be the arbiters of canonical importance, but to show how sustained critical analysis of these texts might bring about a new canon. In addition to their suitability for undergraduate courses, the books will appeal to fans of SFF.

Paul Kincaid

Keith Roberts's
Pavane

A Critical Companion

Paul Kincaid
Folkestone, Kent, UK

ISSN 2662-8562   ISSN 2662-8570   (electronic)
Palgrave Science Fiction and Fantasy: A New Canon
ISBN 978-3-031-71566-2   ISBN 978-3-031-71567-9   (eBook)
https://doi.org/10.1007/978-3-031-71567-9

This Palgrave Macmillan imprint is published by the registered company Springer Nature
Switzerland AG.
The registered company address is: Gewerbestrasse 11, 6330 Cham, Switzerland

If disposing of this product, please recycle the paper.

ACKNOWLEDGEMENTS

A work of this nature is always a collaborative effort, with all sorts of conversations contributing to the finished book. In this instance I want to pay tribute to Christopher Priest and Nina Allan, and to John and Judith Clute, whose long ago conversations steered me towards this book. I also want to thank Sean Rickard, whose question out of the blue sent me down unexpected but profitable pathways. Profound thanks are due also to Roger Robinson for providing a much-needed reference source.

This book is dedicated to the memory of Maureen Kincaid Speller, whose belief, encouragement, and proof reading lie behind everything that may be of value in my writing.

CONTENTS

CHAPTER 1

Introduction: Assembling the Mosaic

Abstract *Pavane* was first published as a sequence of stories in the magazine *Impulse* between March and July 1966, with a further story appearing in *New Worlds* later that year. These were then assembled into a story cycle, with an additional Prologue and Coda, which first appeared in book form in 1968. This chapter examines the origins of the sequence, inspired by an overheard remark on a visit to Corfe. It considers how these stories were assembled and ordered, the role they played in the early career of Keith Roberts, and the initial and continuing response to the book.

Keywords Keith Roberts • *Pavane* • Corfe Castle • *Science Fantasy/SF Impulse*

One day in the early 1960s, Keith Roberts drove down from his home in the Thames Valley to Dorset. It was a trip he made on many occasions; Dorset and the West Country were areas he loved and which would provide a backdrop for much of his fiction. We do not know which, if any, of his various girlfriends accompanied him in his sporty Triumph Spitfire, perhaps the woman he would later call "Lemady". Nor is it known whether the first of his short stories had been published at the time of this trip, possibly not, but it is certain that he already thought of himself as a writer. All

P. Kincaid, *Keith Roberts's* Pavane, Palgrave Science Fiction and Fantasy: A New Canon,
https://doi.org/10.1007/978-3-031-71567-9_1

1

we really know is that he ended up in a pub he frequented in the small town of Corfe.

It was in that pub that he overheard a conversation between another customer and the publican's daughter, a young woman wearing, he noticed, patterned nylons. They were talking about the siege of Corfe Castle during the Civil War. At the time the Royalist defenders were led by the castellan, Lady Mary Bankes, who put up such a stout defence that she won the admiration of the attackers. At one point the barmaid "made a stray remark that she was the reincarnation of Lady Mary, who was the castellan; and I thought, my word, you are" (Kincaid 1986: 5). Roberts had long wanted to write about Corfe Castle, but not in a straightforward historical fiction. The barmaid's remark prompted him to think of a story that married the historic siege with a modern perspective of the castle as a tourist attraction.

That vague idea would become "Corfe Gate", but that story raised questions of its own. In answering those questions, he found himself writing further stories. Before long he had a linked sequence of stories that would become *Pavane*, only his second novel but one that would often be reckoned his most mature and accomplished work.

Keith John Kingston Roberts was born in Kettering, Northants, in 1935. He was the son of a projectionist for Odeon Cinemas and would often visit his father in the projection booth, though he seems to have been more enthralled by the machine his father operated than the flickering stories being projected onto the screen. After grammar school he went to study art before working in a variety of jobs including as a background designer in an animation studio, and in advertising for local newspapers. He had been "playing around with writing off and on for years, usually burning the results about every fourth Saturday" (Roberts 1983: 5). Early attempts to get published were unsuccessful until he was advised to study his market, and having identified the sorts of things he didn't want to write found himself left, seemingly reluctantly, with "what folks for want of a better term call science fiction" (Roberts 1983: 6). What he was interested in writing and what identified his work as science fiction seem to have been two different things. Describing the twentieth century as the age of the pigeonhole, he said: "The particular label attached to me is science fiction writer. I've nothing against it; but I really know very little science. ... I've simply tried to talk about characters who interested me, and events that moved or disturbed me. If that's science fiction, then so be it" (Roberts 1996, 780).

Nevertheless, in science fiction Roberts enjoyed almost immediate success. His first two published stories, "Anita" and "Escapism", would appear in the same issue of *Science Fantasy* (September/October 1964). Earlier that year, *Science Fantasy* and its sister magazine, *New Worlds*, had changed hands, and new editors were now in place, Michael Moorcock at *New Worlds* and Kyril Bonfiglioli at *Science Fantasy*. When Christopher Priest reviewed the new regime at these two magazines, he titled his article with a phrase then popular for everything from French couture to British realist cinema: "New Wave" (Priest 1965: 9). And Roberts was among the few writers he singled out for praise as epitomising this fresh start in science fiction.

Having spent years trying and failing to get into print, Roberts suddenly became prolific. By the end of 1965 he had no fewer than 16 stories in print, not to mention the serialisation of his first novel, *The Furies*. In part this was because, within months of that first sale, he had been appointed associate editor of *Science Fantasy*, and the need to fill 70,000 words a month meant that he produced a lot of stories under his own name and under a variety of pseudonyms. On occasion, he mined his own middle names, John Kingston, for a pseudonym, but mostly these stories appeared as by David Stringer or, more frequently, Alistair Bevan. When, later in his career, he produced *Gráinne* (1987), a novel with a strong autobiographical element, he gave his protagonist the name Alistair Bevan.

Roberts's early fiction varied. On the one hand, there was the whimsy of the Anita stories, tales of a teenage witch in contemporary rural England which featured two characteristics that would become closely identified with his work: a young, independent, tomboyish female character who can be recognised as a precursor of the multigirl (see Chap. 6), and a lovingly delineated setting in the English South West. The Anita stories were consistently popular with readers at the time and were the stories that would invariably appear under his own name. On the other hand, there were more straightforwardly science fictional stories though these too tended to have a contemporary English setting. These would usually pay careful attention to the hands-on everyday mechanics dealing with the various bits of film equipment that feature in "Escapism" (1964), "Boulter's Canaries" (1965), and "Sub-Lim" (1965), or the small town garage finding itself repairing a car fitted with alien technology in "Breakdown" (1966). The setting is determinedly here and now; the characters are people we might encounter anywhere with grease under their fingernails. Given that sense of the mundane, his first novel, *The Furies* (serialised

July–September 1965; volume 1966), seems rather out of step with his other work. Despite the strong tomboyish character of Pete, and the setting that carried the story from Wiltshire to the Mendips, overall the novel was, as Roberts acknowledged, "old fashioned when it was written, quite deliberately so" (letter to the author, 28 April 1987). This is largely because the plot, featuring a landscape torn apart by nuclear tests which set the scene for an invasion by giant alien wasps, was a very conscious revisiting of the sort of catastrophe story John Wyndham had been writing ten years before. It was designed to get him into print, and it worked. Nevertheless, and despite the American publisher who, in response to the manuscript of *The Furies*, declared: "We can take six of these a year" (Kincaid 2008, 174n4), by the time *The Furies* appeared the New Wave had already swept the cosy catastrophe away, and Roberts's writing would never again take such a consciously old-fashioned turn.

But then, by the time Rupert Hart-Davis published the hardback of *The Furies* in 1966, Roberts had met the barmaid in Corfe, had worked out the complicated scenario that she had given him, and had already set his career in a radical new direction.

The little bits of information about the writing of *Pavane* that Roberts gave in various essays and interviews are not always consistent. The most likely sequence of events that we can construct is that he began the novel with "Corfe Gate", the story directly inspired by the barmaid. Nicholas Ruddick quotes Roberts as saying that he then "added the 'Coda' to 'Corfe Gate' before writing the rest of the cycle" (Ruddick 1989: 48, n15). Roberts, however, is not always the most reliable source, and, in this instance, he is clearly mistaken. Because what would become the Coda was, in very different form, an integral part of "Corfe Gate" on its first appearance in the July 1966 issue of *Impulse*. In structural terms, the "Coda", at least as it appears in the book version, is where the notion of cyclical history, implicit throughout the novel, is made explicit. Yet Roberts repeatedly said that "I was guilty ... of changing boats in midstream; I started with the idea of a parallel world, and then decided some cyclical view of history would become useful" (Roberts 1986: 7). This suggestion of a belated switch from alternate history to cyclical history, a switch that Roberts would go on to regret, doesn't quite make sense. The extraneous elements from the magazine appearance of "Corfe Gate", those parts that would be trimmed and extensively revised to form the "Coda", do not spell out the notion of cyclic history to the extent that the Coda does. But there were still hints and references to time repeating itself in that original version of "Corfe Gate", so if not as fully developed as it would be in the book version, the idea of cyclic history was built into the sequence from the very beginning.

"Corfe Gate" clearly concludes the sequence, but along the way there are many oblique and allusive references to a world that we are told is contemporary England but that doesn't feel contemporary. Roberts has said that the mood and feel of the story were derived from "a fine historical writer named Alfred Duggan, who wrote *Leopards and Lilies* [1954], about the internecine warfare between the Normans and the other lot after the conquest. But everyone praised me for originality in that book" (Platt: 184). Therefore, after writing what is effectively an historical story set in the present or near future, the next few stories that Roberts wrote had to go back to fill in the nature of the world. First "The Signaller" explained the semaphore stations; next "The Lady Anne" explained the steam-powered road trains; then "Brother John" turned attention on the role of the Church. The last of this initial set of *Pavane* stories to be written was "Lords and Ladies" which carefully provided the link between "The Lady Anne" and "Corfe Gate". It is obvious that the complete sequence to that point had been written before any of them started to appear in print.

At the beginning of 1966, Kyril Bonfiglioli changed the name of *Science Fantasy*, first to *Impulse* then, after a couple of issues, to *SF Impulse*. Roberts would continue as editor of the magazine, with Harry Harrison as nominal editor-in-chief. But because Harrison spent most of his time out of the country, all of the editorial work devolved on Roberts. Roberts would continue in this role, providing pseudonymously much of the content and all of the cover art until it was absorbed into its sister magazine, *New Worlds*, in March 1967. In the very first issue of *Impulse*, March 1966, Bonfiglioli announced the launch of a new series by Roberts, one that was destined to "establish him firmly in the front rank of imaginative storytellers" (quoted, Peek: 12). The series was *Pavane*, the first story to be published was "The Signaller", and it immediately proved so popular that it encouraged Bonfiglioli to go further, in the July 1966 issue, to declare of Roberts that "I seriously believe that there is no more devoted *craftsman* writing today" (Bonfiglioli: 79).

Published in consecutive issues of the magazine between March and July, the *Pavane* stories immediately attracted what was called, in the introduction to "Corfe Gate", an "unprecedented spate of letters from readers" (Roberts 1966: 7). So much so that Michael Moorcock specifically commissioned another story in the same vein for *New Worlds*. The immediate inspiration for that story, "The White Boat", came with "a weekend's cruising on a magnificent ninety-foot racing yacht" (Roberts 1986: 6). Though Roberts has also suggested that this wasn't exactly an enjoyable experience, and the captain was something of a martinet. Nevertheless, the story it inspired was one of the more striking of the *Pavane* sequence, and would appear in the December 1966 issue of *New Worlds*.

The five original stories were brought together as a book from Rupert Hart-Davis in 1968. The American edition, from Doubleday, which came out later the same year, also included "The White Boat", though it was in the wrong position in the sequence. It would not be until the Penguin edition of the book in 1984 that "The White Boat" was included in a British volume, and in the right position in the sequence.

Pavane was praised from the moment it appeared. In his review, Christopher Priest called it "a magnificent, miraculous novel" (Priest 1968: 15), while in *Galaxy* Algis Budrys called it "a marvelous work. A truly marvelous work" (Budrys 1985: 207), and later expanded on this to say it was an impressive literary achievement "whose very structure and style were in exact harmony with its theme. Episodic, moody and picked out in elaborate detail" (Budrys 1985: 298). Later commentators have echoed such praise. For David Langford, "[T]he man is a magician with a feel for myth and a feel for words. ... His vision floods the work with colour, contrasting sharply with the black-and-white efforts of lesser men" (Langford: 31–33). Dave Hutchinson insists, "At the height of his powers—and I'd submit that *Pavane* represented the apogee of his work—Roberts was a wonderful writer" (Hutchinson: n.p.). And M. John Harrison considers, "We are used to Roberts as an exemplar ... [and some of his stories] ... remain some of the sharpest templates we have for a mature science fiction" (Bould & Reid: 137).

Yet despite the admiration that his work continues to attract from his fellow writers, few if any of the histories of science fiction that have appeared in the nearly 40 years since *Trillion Year Spree* by Brian Aldiss with David Wingrove (1986) have even mentioned his name, and he is almost entirely absent from other surveys of the genre. He is, in Nina Allan's words, "one of the most underappreciated talents in British science fiction" (Allan: 69). This may be a consequence of the work itself; Charles Platt describes *Pavane*, along with the other books that are acknowledged as among his best, as falling "somewhere in that awkward area that lies outside the everyday world of modern literature, not quite in the techno-logical territory of science fiction, but beyond the pure wish-fulfillment of modern fantasy" (Platt: 174). This may explain, he implies, why Roberts can be critically acclaimed without attracting wider recognition.

Regrettably, another explanation may lie with the man himself. In his obituary of Roberts, Jim Goddard declares that he was one of the finest writers to emerge from British science fiction in the second half of the twentieth century, but at the same time notes that he was incapable of friendship, someone who distrusted everyone on principle, and fell out with everyone who became close to him. For my part, I recall one of the leading figures in British science fiction publishing assuring me that the work which would become *Gráinne* and which would go on to win the BSFA Best Novel Award and be shortlisted for the Arthur C. Clarke Award was unpublishable. I think this was a polite way of saying that it was impossible for any publisher to work with Roberts. He even managed to fall out with the friends who established Kerosina Publications for the express purpose of publishing, first, *Kaeti & Company* (1986) and then *Gráinne*.

Be that as it may, the fact remains that *Pavane* is an incredibly rich and complex work, vivid, colourful, open to a host of interpretations, and wor-thy of being visited and revisited regularly. In this short book I hope to point readers towards just some of the features and characteristics that made *Pavane* so intriguing and fascinating for readers from the word go. Thus, after laying out the structure of the book, I will examine the tech-nological world presented, the multifaceted religious interplay at work within the stories, the vital importance of landscape, and, finally, briefly, look at the way art underlies the construction of the world and introduce the character of the multigirl who would go on to be one of the most interesting and important characters in his later work.

BIBLIOGRAPHY

KEITH ROBERTS

"Comment". 1996. *St. James Guide to Science Fiction Writers: Fourth Edition*. Edited by Jay P. Pederson. New York: St James Press, 780.
"Corfe Gate" (Original Version). 1966. *Impulse* 1 (5): 7–68.
Gráinne. 1987. Salisbury: Kerosina Publications.

Introduction. 1983. *British Science Fiction Writers: Keith Roberts.* Edited by Paul
    Kincaid and Geoff Rippington. Folkestone: British Science Fiction
    Association, 5–6.
Kaeti & Company. 1986. Salisbury: Kerosina Publications.
Pavane. 1968 [1985]. London: Penguin.
The Chalk Giant: Reflections by Keith Roberts. 1986. *Vector* 132 (June/July): 6–8.
The Furies. 1966. London: Rupert Hart-Davis.

SECONDARY SOURCES

Allan, Nina. 2018. The Fourfold Library (8): Keith Roberts, *Pavane. Foundation*
    131: 69–71.
Bonfiglioli, Kyril. 1966. Editorial. *Impulse* Vol. 1, Issue 5: 2–3, 79.
Bould, Mark, and Michelle Reid, eds. 2005. *Parietal Games: Critical Writings by
    and on M. John Harrison.* London: Science Fiction Foundation; Foundation
    Studies in Science Fiction 5.
Budrys, Algis. 1985. *Benchmarks: Galaxy Bookshelf.* Carbondale: Southern Illinois
    University Press.
Hutchinson, Dave. 2016. Science Fiction in Your Own Back Yard: *Pavane* by
    Keith Roberts. *Reactor.* https://reactormag.com/science-fiction-in-your-
    own-back-yard-pavane-by-keith-roberts/. Accessed 15 April 2024.
Kincaid, Paul. 1986. A Mosaic of Words. *Vector* 132 (June/July): 2–5.
———. 2008. The Furies. In *What It Is We Do When We Read Science Fiction,*
    173–187, Harold Wood: Beccon Publications.
Langford, David. 2003. *Up Through an Empty House of Stars. Reviews and Essays
    1980–2002.* Holicong, PA: Cosmos Books.
Peek, Bernie. 1986. Exercises in Landscape. *Vector* 132 (June/July): 12–13.
Platt, Charles. 1982. *Dream Makers: Volume II.* Strange Particle Press. Revised
    edition: 2021.
Priest, Christopher. 1965. New Wave—Prozines. *Zenith Speculation* 8
    (March): 9–11.
———. 1968. Death of a Faery Queen. *Vector* 51 (October): 15–16, 21.
Ruddick, Nicholas. 1989. Flaws in the Timestream: Unity and Disunity in Keith
    Roberts's Story-Cycles. *Foundation* 45 (Spring): 38–49.

CHAPTER 2

Measures of the Dance

Abstract This chapter considers the structure of *Pavane*, a work that has
at different times been considered both a novel and a short story collection. The other controversial issue connected to *Pavane* is whether to
think of it as an alternate history or as cyclic history; neither seems to
adequately encompass the work. After discussing these issues, the chapter
goes on to lay out in some detail the contents of the book, setting out the
key incidents described in each of the six central stories and how the different stories echo and react to each other, along with the more problematic aspects of the Prologue and the Coda.

Keywords Story cycle • Mosaic novel • Alternate history •
Cyclic history

How we should refer to the finished work, *Pavane*, has been a matter of
some dispute over the years. As Roberts himself insisted, speaking of both
Pavane and a structurally similar later work, *The Chalk Giants* (1974),
"They're not novels, and were never intended to be" (Kincaid 1982: 11),
but neither is it a collection of otherwise disconnected stories. The problem with this structure is that, instead of the unity of plot and continuity
of character that we might expect of a novel, "we are given instead a text
characterized by fragmentation, discontinuity and absence" (Ruddick

P. Kincaid, *Keith Roberts's* Pavane, Palgrave Science Fiction and
Fantasy: A New Canon,
https://doi.org/10.1007/978-3-031-71567-9_2

9

1990: 37). Hence various descriptions have been applied to the work: "fragmented novel" (Mike Ashley), "mosaic novel" (myself and Nicholas Ruddick), Nina Allan talks of "interlaced stories" (Allan: 69) that form "interlocking parts of an inalienable whole" (Allan: 71). Roberts himself tended to think of it as a story cycle, but in "Corfe Gate" he has Lady Eleanor lay out the pattern of the book to her fairy seneschal, Sir John, when she says:

> It's like a ... dance somehow, a minuet or a pavane. Something stately and pointless, with all its steps set out. With a beginning and an end ... life's all a mass of significance, all sorts of strands and threads woven like a tapestry or a brocade. So if you pulled one out or broke it the pattern would alter right back through the cloth. Then I think ... it's all totally pointless, it would make just as much sense backwards as forwards, effects lead to causes and those to more effects ... maybe that's what will happen when we get to the end of Time. The whole world will shoot undone like a spring, and wind itself back to the start. (212–13)

Each of the stories that make up *Pavane* is described as a Measure, a step in the dance. Even if we don't think of the work as a novel, the image presented here, a stately dance in which each movement is strictly prescribed, a tightly woven tapestry, suggests that the whole is far more carefully integrated, each measure positioned so it makes sense forwards and backwards, than any emphasis on the separateness of the stories would allow.

Thus, as we look at each measure in turn, we have to consider it not as a distinct individual piece, but as a congeries of threads each of which is tied to every other measure. The power of the book lies not in a simple story, but in the accumulation of details which, as Ruddick puts it, focus on "the process whereby society emerges from feudalism into enlightenment, with science and technology as the agent of transformation" (Ruddick 1989b: 15). That process is slow and cumulative, hence the sequence extends over three generations at least. We look between different individuals from different levels of society each slowly coming to challenge authority. Step by step in the dance we explore how the various influences that make us—traditions, desires, hopes—can combine to make us reject the suffocating rigidity of an all-powerful state. The various characters in the six measures of the dance all stand for something, and all are knocked down, three of them, indeed, are killed. But the fact of standing has unexpected consequences further down the line. It is a perspective that rejects the Judeo-Christian linear temporality of aspirations towards heaven in favour of a more ancient view of time as a great wheel. The weapons in this war between aspiration and authority are beliefs; the Catholic Church triumphant becomes the villain of the piece simply by standing in the way of other belief systems that encourage individuality.

In time, Roberts would come to regard *Pavane* as "hung around my neck like the traditional albatross" because, as he acknowledged, it was "an early book and very far from faultless" (Roberts 1986: 6). This discontent, I suspect, was largely down to the role assigned to the Catholic Church (see Chap. 4). Although Roberts insisted that he was neither pro nor anti-religion—"My great Church lunges and plunges, baffled; but it isn't evil. I tried to make that plain" (Roberts 1986: 7)—it was a convenient fall guy. As he admitted, "I was rather sorry when I did *Pavane*, I felt I'd dragged the Catholic Church in by the scruff of its neck, screaming" (Kincaid 1986: 5), something he tried to repair in later works, most notably *The Chalk Giants*.

Another argument would have it that the flaw lies in the two parts that have only ever been published in the book version, the Prologue and Coda which according to Ruddick, "actually damage the thematic unity of what lies between them" (Ruddick 1989b: 16). These are the two parts, the Coda in particular, that make explicit the cyclic nature of time. Without them, *Pavane* could be read (almost) as a straightforward alternate history, which indeed is how the work is most commonly identified. According to Darko Suvin, alternate history is "that form of SF in which an alternative locus (in space, time, etc.) that shares the material and causal verisimilitude of the writer's world is used to articulate different possible solutions of societal problems, these problems being of sufficient importance to require an alteration in the overall history of the narrated world" (Suvin: 149). Jim Clarke further suggests that alternate histories challenge "our preconceived assumptions about the march of history, eroding its sense of deterministic inevitability" (Clarke: 202). Read as alternate history, therefore, *Pavane* suggests that Catholic domination might have retarded both technological and social advance, rendering fragile our familiar modern world. But the Coda tells us something else; here we learn that there were no concentration camps, that many of the horrors of the twentieth century were thus avoided. This new information does not fit within an alternate history scenario, because if the concentration camps never happened in this reality, there would be no knowledge of them. It is clumsily done, the only really clumsy part of the book, because it is addressed to the reader not to the inhabitants of this world, but it makes clear that this is a case of cyclic rather than alternate history.

But if the Coda is a flaw, it is not damaging in the way that Ruddick suggests. Because cyclic history is not some second thoughts that Roberts dumped into the book only at the last minute. The Coda may be where the idea of cyclic history is spelled out, rather too broadly, but it is not new to the Coda. Anyone reading the book with even a modicum of attention would have seen references to cyclic history crop up all the way through. It is there in the last dying visions of Rafe and of John; it is there, quite explicitly, in "Lords and Ladies" when one of the Old Ones tells Margaret: "The dream ... is ending. If it is a dream. The great Dance finishes, another will begin" (148); it is there when Eleanor talks to John the Seneschal about the pavane in the passage quoted above. If there is a flaw in *Pavane* it is not to be found in the Prologue and Coda, for both play an essential part in establishing and understanding the world we see as we tread the measures of the dance.

The Prologue, written, I suspect, as the stories were being prepared for volume publication, sets out the history of this other England in a way that is never quite made explicit in any of the individual stories. It sets this up brutally in the very first sentence: "On a warm July evening of the year 1588, in the royal palace of Greenwich, London a woman lay dying, an assassin's bullets lodged in abdomen and chest" (7). Queen Elizabeth's premature death allows the approaching Armada to defeat England. In two staccato sentences we learn that Philip of Spain became the ruler of England, the House of Valois is overthrown in France, and the last of the Wars of Religion in France ends with "the Church restored once more to her ancient power" (7). Thus, the forces of the counter-Reformation destroy the rising Protestant powers of the Netherlands and Germany, North America remains under Spanish rule, and "Cook planted in Australasia the cobalt flag of the Throne of Peter" (8).

Roberts positions England as "a land half ancient and half modern" a land "haunted by things dead and others best forgotten; bears and cata-mounts, dire wolves and Fairies" (8). The emphasis here is on the historic, the legendary, the supernatural. The England we are introduced to in the following stories feels more of the past than of the present. Except that "[r]ebellion was once more in the air" (8), the final words of the Prologue, spell out that all that follows is primarily about resistance, dissent, rebellion.

That backward look is even more explicit in the first measure, "The Lady Anne", here retitled "The Lady Margaret". (I have not seen Roberts anywhere explain this change of title. My guess is that the Lady Anne, with its apparent reference back to Anne Boleyn, "The Protestant Whore" as she was called, and the mother of Queen Elizabeth, might have been politically dodgy in a world where all signs of Protestantism are ruthlessly suppressed.) The story is dated "1968", and located at "Durnovaria", the Roman name for the city that became Dorchester. Roman names like this, and other places mentioned throughout the story cycle, like Isca (Exeter), or Camulodunum (Colchester), or Sorviodunum (Salisbury), or Londinium, had fallen out of use centuries before Elizabeth, so their use here indicates that the assassination of Elizabeth was not a changing point in history, but rather supports the idea of a cyclic history.

It is mid-December, and Jesse Strange, who has just become head of the Strange road haulage business following the death of his father, Eli, is readying an engine for the last run of the year. The engine, called "The Lady Margaret", is the pride of the Strange fleet, a Burrell, that is, it was built by Charles Burrell & Sons, specialists in building traction engines who, in our world, were in business in Thetford, Norfolk, from 1770 to 1928, though some of their engines are still in operation today. In the world of *Pavane*, of course, they are still in business, because although there are more modern technologies available, they are limited. The Papal Bull, *Petroleum Veto*, issued in 1910, had limited the capacity of internal combustion engines to 150cc. Petrol vehicles had been forced to fit gaudy sails to help move them along, hence the nickname "butterfly cars" (16). Their limited capacity meant they were useless for road haulage and were treated with contempt by the hauliers. There are oil burners available for the road trains but they have not been blessed by the Church. So although Eli would have eagerly fitted them "and damned the priests black to their faces" he could not because his employees "would have baulked at the excommunication that would certainly have followed" (27). Already we see that the proto-capitalists of the age are growing increasingly discontent with the restrictive rule of the Church. The stasis introduced by the Church had not been good for business, particularly when we realise that "gold, stacked anywhere but in the half-legendary coffers of the Vatican, meant danger" (15). So, the rise of businesses like the Stranges threatened to take gold away from the Church, and so made them vulnerable to attack from the Church. The tension seen here that will eventually manifest in rebellion actually runs both ways.

This modern England is not a safe place: "This was the twentieth century, the age of reason; but the heath was still the home of superstitious fears. The haunt of wolves and witches, were-things and Fairies" (22). Jesse's route to the coast takes him past a number of strongholds that had been built because "there had been enough revolts in the country to teach caution even to the Popes" (23). And of course this mid-winter journey is particularly risky because it is the time when the *routiers* or highwaymen are particularly active. The growing revolt that is traced throughout the course of *Pavane* does not come out of the blue.

Jesse's outward journey to Swanage goes safely enough, but there he meets Margaret, the barmaid, after whom he had named the *Lady Margaret*, the first appearance in the fiction of the Corfe barmaid who had prompted this story cycle. When he declares his love for her, she gently but firmly turns him down. It is in that mood of bitter rejection that he begins his return journey to Durnovaria, when he is unexpectedly joined by Colin de la Haye, the rakish figure who had been his best friend at college. Col is a *routier*, and Jesse carefully directs him and his gang to the riches carried in the last waggon. These riches consist of "two score kegs of fine-grain powder packed round with bricks and scrap iron" (47–8) which he had loaded before he even set out from Durnovaria. As Jesse springs his trap and "scythed the valley clear of life" (48), the story concludes: "The firm of Strange had not been built on softness; what you stole from it, you were welcome to keep" (48).

The second measure, and the first of the stories to have seen print, "The Signaller", focuses on two of the most important features of this world, features that will re-appear again and again throughout the measures of the dance: the network of semaphore signal stations and the Fairies.

The story opens with Rafe lying badly injured in the snow outside his lonely and isolated signal station. He has been badly mauled by a wildcat, and now, weak, bloody, and in pain, he wants to "just stay quiet and be dead" (52). Nevertheless, by some extreme effort of will, he manages to get back to his semaphore station where he collapses into unconsciousness.

At some point while he is unconscious a Fairy girl materialises in the station to look after him. Also while unconscious he has a flashback to his childhood and his induction into the Guild of Signallers. Given that the Fairies are explicitly linked with time, we might assume that the two are not coincidental. Certainly, Rafe's initial fascination with the semaphore station on Silbury Hill is explicitly linked to his similar fascination with the standing stones and ancient barrows of Avebury. We get our first suggestion that there are connections between the Signallers and the Fairies, a suggestion that will be made clearer in later stories, when we learn that the Serjeant of Signals who first encounters Rafe "knows about Time, that Time is forever and scurry and bustle can wait" (57), a formulation that is echoed when the Fairy is telling Rafe stories of a distant past when "Nothing had existed but Time; Time, and a void. Only Time was the void, and the void was Time" (77).

We also learn that the Signallers have a level of independence within the system that no other body does. They are vital both for governance and for business, and so their codes are jealously guarded, and they "paid no tithes to local demesnes, obeyed none but their own hierarchy; and though in theory they were answerable under common law, in practice they were immune" (59). More significantly, as we learn later in "Corfe Gate", "for centuries the Guild of Signallers had enjoyed privileges not even the Popes dared question" (178). The Signallers don't just guard this independence, they exploit it.

Powerful as they are, the Signallers carefully control entry to the Guild. Rafe is from a poor family, and so must negotiate entry to the College of Signals which allocates only 12 places a year for Common Entrants. His success means subjecting himself to an intense and gruelling training course, which ends with a graduation test so arduous that Rafe "felt disembodied; he could sense his limbs only as a dim and confused burning" (69). This mirrors the transformative effect on Brother John of witnessing torture, the characters become themselves only through pain, through loss of self. We see this coming into oneself through a form of disembodiment as one of the persistent motifs throughout the book: Jesse reacting to Margaret's rejection, Becky's orgasmic experience in swimming towards the White Boat.

When Rafe comes to in his semaphore station it is to find a girl that he recognises as "one of the Old Ones, the half-believed, the Haunters of the Heath, the possessors of men's souls if Mother Church spoke truth" (76). Immediately we are outwith the authority of the Church, and when she sings to him of Norns and Yggdrasil, he "knew the girl was mad, or possessed. She spoke of Old things, the things banished by Mother Church, pushed out for ever into the dark and cold" (77). Under her influence he has a vision of the distant past and a land that is itself alive: "The hills shuddered, drew back, thrust up again like golden, humped animals, shaking the water from their sides ... [and from this living land emerge the old Gods] ... springing from the silt, sinking back to silt again, the hills writhed, shaping the shapeless land" (78). The vision encompasses the story of creation, the formation of the land, the herds of animals that crossed the land, the emergence of men, the coming of the ice, a void of "coldness and blackness and nothingness and winter" (79) into which appeared Balder, who is not the Christos of Mother Church but must play the same role, killed upon the tree Yggdrasil, and "from His blood sprang warmth again and grass and sunlight, the meadow flowers and the calling, mating birds" (79). Only now does the Church come at last, accompanied by wars and bloodshed, and claim for their own Christos all that was true of Balder. Roberts adapts the myth of Balder, the "shining one" of Norse mythology, for his own ends. In most versions of the myth, Balder was killed by a dart made from mistletoe, but later tales, building on a reference in *Beowulf*, have him dying on a gallows tree, like Woden (Davidson: 189), enough for others beside Roberts to try to equate him with Christ though such attempts "seem wholly unfounded" (Jordan: 45). Nevertheless, this equation is central to what the Fairies have to relate, and Rafe's vision mirrors John's vision of the distant future in the moment of his death. Look closely, and there is much mirroring between one measure of this dance and the next.

And the story comes at last to the present, where the Fairy girl tells Rafe he is better now and leads him outside into the coming of spring. When horsemen from the Signallers arrive just days after the semaphore station had gone silent (so still in winter, not the spring that Rafe had walked into), they find the hut is neatly maintained, everything in its place, but "everywhere, the Fairy mark danced across the wood" (81). They are left to wonder "What did [the Fairies] look like, when they came? What did they talk of, in locked cabins to dying men?" (82).

The third measure, "Brother John", has so many points in common with "The Signaller" that it feels like a counterpoint to the earlier story. Like Rafe, John comes from a poor background, so there is an understated class tension underlying the dissent we see. And as Rafe's fascination with the signal station renders him unfit to be apprenticed to a tailor, so John's artistic inclinations render him unfit to follow the family trade as a cobbler. So the only place for John is the monastery of St Adhelm, where we first discover him working on an advertising poster for Harvesters Ale, which is brewed by the monks. Once again, dissent has a connection to commerce.

As in "The Lady Margaret", dissent is also tied to dissatisfaction with restrictions on technology, though again it is remarkably low-key technology that is at issue. Here the tympans, used to equalise pressure in the printing process, were greased with bear fat, whose stink offended John. So he had "scrounge[d] from the town's one garage a tin of the newfangled mineral grease, with which he had anointed the presses" (89). The newness is not welcomed by the church authorities (though we note that while the monastery's accountant is inscribing his records by hand on rolls of parchment, the Abbot has a typewriter in his office) and John finds himself subject to penances. It is presumably as much because he is an irritant as because of his skill that John is considered the ideal choice to serve as an "artist" (the Abbot uses the word with obvious distaste) for the Inquisition.

The Court of Spiritual Welfare, the Inquisition, is situated in Dover Castle, here called Dubris. John's assignment is "to record, for the benefit of Rome, all stages in the procedure of the Court of Father Hieronymous, Witchfinder in General to Pope John" (95). (The actual pope at the time the novel was written, and set, was Paul VI; Pope John XXIII had died in 1963. The fact that Roberts has given the same name to his dissident and to the pope is suggestive of a duality of character.) As John approaches the torture chamber for the first time, "his face screwed up as if in anticipation of pain" (96). When John questions the principles behind the Inquisition, he excuses himself on the grounds that "we Adhelmians are technicians and mechanics, mere journeymen not noted in our lower orders at least for learning of such profundity" (97). Again we get the distinction between the technical and the religious, which is why dissent when it comes is from the technical and commercial classes.

John's experience of the Inquisition is marked by a perverse ecstasy: "The brilliant side lighting; film of sweat on bodies that distended and heaved in ecstasies of pain; arms disjointed by the weights and pulleys, stomachs exploded by the rack, bright tree shapes of new blood running to the floor. It seemed the limner tried to force the stench, the squalor, even at last the noise down onto paper" (98/9). In the end, all he can say about the experience is: "I *enjoyed* it, Brother ... God and the Saints preserve me, *I enjoyed my work*" (99). As he left Dubris he deliberately dropped his satchel of brushes and paints into a stream: after what he had seen there could be no more art. And when finally he silently quits his own monastery, he has lost weight, his clothes are frayed, he stares blankly ahead, vacant-faced; in some ways he mirrors Rafe at the opening of "The Signaller", which is appropriate since this, too, is a prefiguring of visions and of death.

John becomes an itinerant preacher, viewed by the Church authorities as a renegade who is rousing the countryside to insurgency. The Cardinal Archbishop of Londinium had himself excommunicated John, but this had only aroused his followers more, their response including killing a detachment of troops and burning the Pope "in effigy at Woodhenge and Badbury Rings" (102), their rebellion here associated with ancient monuments, and the "resurging power of Anglicanism fed on such relics of ancient worship" (103).

As the rebellion spreads, we learn that Bible texts translated into English are placed on Church alters, which suggests that the rebellion is seen as the English rising up against a foreign oppressor. And there is the hint of ancient ways, ancient beliefs, underlying it all; John is rumoured to meet with Fairies "by the stones of temples old before the Romans came" (108). This tie to antiquity (though it is not clear whether Romans here refers to the legions or to Roman Catholicism) is made explicit when John watches a blind quarryman working himself to death and realises that "[t]he Old gods would have understood ... [and the Christian God] ... is the same. His drink is blood. His food is flesh. His sacraments work and misery and endless hopeless pain" (113). This echoes the linking of Christ and Balder in "The Signaller", and there is another parallel in John's final vision which turns, this time, to the future, or perhaps, as some have argued, to our reality outside the novel. He describes a Golden Age

> rising about him on the hills, the buildings of that new time, the factories and hospitals, power stations and laboratories. He saw the machines flying above the land, skimming like bubbles the surface of the sea. He saw wonders; lightning chained, the wild waves of the very air made to talk and sing. ... The age of tolerance, of reason, of humanity, of the dignity of the human soul. (116)

And like Rafe, John now disappears from life.

If "The Signaller" and "Brother John" mirror each other, so the fourth measure, "Lords and Ladies", echoes the first. Just as "The Lady Margaret" began with the death of Eli Strange, so "Lords and Ladies" begins with Eli's heir, Jesse Strange, on his deathbed, a scene that the story returns to repeatedly throughout its length. The story revolves around the dubious interactions of commerce, aristocracy, and the Church, each as we see mistrusting the others. The priest in attendance at Jesse's deathbed, for instance, is not comforting the dying but conducting an exorcism: "I exorcize thee, most vile spirit … flee from this creature of God" (121). Creature of God is hardly an apt description of Jesse, who is every bit as hard as Eli and who sees work as "a sacrament, a panacea for all ills" (125).

The scene is being witnessed by Margaret, the second iteration of the Corfe barmaid, and the first of the three women who are central to the last three measures of this dance. We learn, obliquely, that this Margaret's mother had been the daughter of a pub landlord out Portland way, who had married Tim Strange, Jesse's brother, after her father died. The marriage had resulted in Tim being cast out of the family, but that Margaret had then run off with "my Lord of Purbeck's *jongleur*" (128), so Tim had returned to the family with his new daughter, "and Jesse had laughed quiet and long, and made over to him the half of his business" (128).

Like Jesse, Margaret does not conform to the state religion. She "held her tongue at confession" (122) and is aware of practices of the old religion among the country folk, the "furrows where bread and other things were buried in defiance of Mother Church" (123). And there is an emphasis on Time that, recalling Rafe's final moments, links Margaret to the Fairies. For instance, "once the landing reeled under Margaret, an accident of Time maybe that let her see flitting ahead the *doppelganger*, shadow of herself, alien in the warm night" (129–30). And Margaret wonders to herself, could "the Things that knocked and fretted, the haunters, *the Old Ones* … Snatch her out of Space and Time" (131). In fact, the whole story is visionary in its way, told through memories and daydreams as Margaret sits beside Jesse's deathbed, each subsequent memory being presented as Margaret scurrying forward through time. At New Year's Eve, Margaret "wanted to cry for the passing of Time and all transient things" (142), and later, as she sits by Jesse's deathbed and recalls her affair with Robert, her vision changes, "From the past she had moved to the future, or to some Time that had never been and never would be" (146). And here she encounters a stranger who declares: "Who calls on the Old Ones, calls on me" (146).

Robert is the Lord of Purbeck, heir to Corfe Castle, an arrogant nobleman who believes he has the right to bed any common woman he wishes. When he first takes Margaret to Corfe he hands her over to a maid with the dehumanising instruction: "*Do* something with it. … Take it off and bathe it or something, before it starts to sneeze" (135). But Margaret is a Strange, and there is nothing common about her. She puzzled Robert because "[s]he wasn't of his blood; but neither did she think like a commoner … She didn't blush and simper, giggle like a village slut when he stroked her breasts; she was grave and quiet and always it seemed had some sadness in her eyes" (142/3). Nevertheless, after sleeping with him she knows that "she'd sold herself for a pretty song ... that a Lord of Purbeck would never mix his blood with a girl of the rank and file" (144). And she cannot get revenge because "there was no law in this land, not for commoners" (145). But this awakening allows Margaret to see the inequality in the land, so the priest continues to torment Jesse with his exorcism because "he like the Church he serves is blind and empty and vainglorious" (145). So, Margaret decides "I'll go out and look for other gods, and maybe they'll be better and anyway they can't be worse" (145). Awareness of class differences, of social inequalities, is thus equated with seeking out another god. Significantly, when Margaret wants to insult Robert she calls him "*Fils de pretre ...*" (133), son of a priest.

Later, in "Corfe Gate", we learn that Margaret and Robert did get together again, but "Lords and Ladies" ends, as so many of the measures do, with defeat and disappointment and, of course, the death of Jesse. Because this is a work about revolution, and the seeds of revolution so frequently lie in such discontents.

As I have indicated, the first four measures interact with each other, reflect upon each other, in curious and interesting ways. But the fifth measure, the one that was written six months or more after the rest, does not have that intimate connection to its fellows. It does add to the cumulative light that is being cast upon this other England, but at the same time it feels somewhat disconnected from the rest. It is, therefore, possible to see why it was originally excluded from the UK edition of *Pavane*, but was rather included in the short story collection, *The Grain Kings* (1976), because of all the measures it is the one that best stands alone as a story. Nevertheless, it is valuable to see "The White Boat" within the context of the story cycle as a whole.

What "The White Boat" brings to the sequence is an awareness of something outside England. The other measures in the dance present an England (and it is always an England; history took its divergent course before the union of the thrones, and so neither Scotland, nor indeed any other constituent parts of Great Britain, appears in the story) almost hermetically sealed off from the rest of the world. The only foreign influence is the Church. But in "The White Boat", suddenly, there is an outside world, and if not particularly benevolent, it is considerably less malevolent than the Church. Indeed, there is a suggestion that nowhere else, even within the Catholic realm, is as restricted, either technologically or socially, as England.

The White Boat, the visitant from another world, is visibly different from the entire experience of our protagonist, Becky. Her world is black, coloured, possessed by the exposed coal seam. When her mother dies of a lung disease we suspect is an effect of the black air, "Becky knew the earth had taken her to squeeze and squeeze, make her into more black shale" (159). There is no escape from this all-encompassing blackness; even at sea the lobsters are "black and slate-grey as the cliffs", the bait is "grey-white rags of bait", the basket is tarred (153). Only the White Boat offers any contrast, as if it was "nothing but a vision or a dream, lacking weight and substance" (156). So much of *Pavane* is about dreams and visions.

When men from the boat buy her lobsters with real gold coins her father is angry, calling the boat *The Bermudan*, a name suggestive of somewhere distant, though the name is never used again. But disapproval doesn't stop her becoming obsessed with the boat, which in her dreams she links with approaching adulthood. She cuts her black hair short. She learns to swim, something neither her father nor the Church would approve of. And when the morning comes when she will swim out to the boat the thought seemed "to cut her off from earthly contact" (160). At that moment the village is "black, lightless, and dead", the sky "dark as pitch", the church "black and remote" (160), but as she swims out to the light of the boat she feels "something that was nearly an orgasm" (161). In the confusion as she is brought on board the White Boat she glimpses "glaring red", so when one of the yachtsmen refers to her as a "bloody fisher-girl" (161) it is both dismissive and, possibly, descriptive. The dream of her first period may have become a reality.

Aboard the White Boat really is a different world in which Becky does not belong. Meals are prepared with unknown spices and relishes; she is seasick; she overhears the crew arguing about whether to kill her. But she is taken to drink wine in a waterfront bar in France, the only one of the central characters in *Pavane* to set foot on a foreign shore, and when she is returned to England she is presented with bottles of alcohol intended as bribes for her father. Along the way she realises that the boat is engaged in smuggling. She comes upon a "slim oil-cloth packet … not much bigger than the boxes of lucifers she bought sometimes in the village shop" (168) and when she examines it, she senses "the heretical smell … of wax and bakelite and brass" (170). We never know exactly what is being smuggled though the bakelite and brass suggest that it wouldn't be unfamiliar in the

1960s when Roberts was writing this story. All we do know is that it is seemingly readily available in Catholic Europe; only in restrictive England does it give off the whiff of "heresies that stopped her breath" (168).

On her return to the black heart of her village, Becky is beaten by her father, and when she shows the device she had stolen to the village priest, the place is immediately filled with soldiers. They are there in part to impose a curfew because once before the villagers had rebelled behind Brother John, but they are also laying a trap for the White Boat. But Becky, having a change of heart, slips out in the night and manages to spring the trap, and "White Boat, turning, laughed at the guns" (174).

In purely literary terms, "The White Boat" is probably the best of the stories that make up *Pavane*. But in structural terms it contradicts much of what we learn elsewhere in the sequence. In particular, by suggesting that England has been treated differently from the rest of the Catholic world, it undermines the excuses for the behaviour of the Church that are offered in the Coda.

But for now we must turn back to the very beginning of the sequence. The final measure, "Corfe Gate", is the first story written, the direct expression of the idea presented by the barmaid in Corfe, who does herself appear here in her third iteration. In fact she takes on the role that her casual remark sparked in Roberts, Lady Eleanor: the modern day castellan of Corfe Castle in patterned stockings.

Eleanor is the only child of Robert and Margaret (from "Lords and Ladies") after they were reconciled. Margaret who died in childbirth was said to be beloved of the Fairies, who are rumoured to have assisted in her conception; Eleanor made no attempt to scotch those rumours. When her father died, Eleanor became the mistress of Corfe. Since she is also the last of the Strange family whose taxes form a significant proportion of the Crown's income, she avoids being married off to some other noble and holds on to her inheritance. Eleanor's alliance with the Fairies (through her seneschal and, we suspect, lover, John Faulkner) and her family connection to the Strange business makes for a dual heritage of independence from the established order. And it is that heritage that makes her conscious of the poverty and hardship affecting the people within her realm: she "seemed to identify herself more with the ordinary people of the countryside than with those of her own rank; which in a way was understandable considering that she was only partly of noble blood" (188). As she says to John Faulkner, "As long as the Church applies a censorship to certain forms of progress, which is what she does however strenuously the Popes deny it, we shall always be a scrappy little nation living just above the famine line" (191). The seeds of rebellion have been sown. And with this comes a resentment of the Church: the local Father Sebastian is seen as both pious and mean, as if the two are synonyms. "He'd walk miles in the snow to pray for a sick child, he's a very good man; but if there was more money about to start with maybe the child wouldn't have been taken ill" (192). This stance is echoed in her espousal of radical new ideas. She has a generator installed in the castle to provide light and heat, an heretical act since "although the principles of the electro-motive force had been known for many years the Church had never sanctioned its domestic use" (194).

Everything we have seen so far indicative of a growing discontent throughout the country is embodied within Eleanor: the desire for technological progress regardless of whether it has been approved by the Church or not; the resentment of the alienness of the Church; the identification with ordinary people and old ways; the alliance with the Fairies. To this we can add an alliance with the Signallers, who we have already seen are associated with the Fairies. Thus when the Signaller Captain brings word that the Archbishop of Londinium has set out for Purbeck with a force of 70 men, it doesn't just reveal that the Signallers are on her side, it also lets slip that they have another, faster means of communication, which they deem "necromancy" (196) but which is really radio. This growing rebellion against the authority of the Church is in part a revolt of the old ways and beliefs against the Church, but equally it is a revolt of the modern against the old, and of the native against the foreign. To Eleanor, she is loyal to King Charles over the Church: "I'm getting so tired of strangers lording it over England, even if it is heresy to say so" (197).

All of this comes to a head with a new tax assessment, when an additional levy on grain is imposed upon Dorset, a levy that would lead to severe hunger within the county. So she refuses to pay. Her disaffection is displayed in her debate with the Archbishop of Londinium when she enumerates medical advances—caesarean sections, anaesthetics, disinfectants—that are forbidden by the Church: "Are we to learn from this, it is better to die of holiness than live in heresy?" (200). And when the Archbishop, in reply, talks of the charity of the Pope, she responds: "[T]he Church is fast forgetting the meaning of the word" (200) because of the levy on the food that her people need to live.

This refusal to pay taxes puts Eleanor in open rebellion against the authority of the Church, and she faces escalating challenges. The Archbishop of Londinium fails to persuade her. Then the Provost of

England arrives as a friend and treacherously tries to capture her. She escapes on a passing steam engine, "A great worn-out wreck she was, ending her days hauling wood and manure and stone, but still liveried in the dark maroon of Strange and Sons" (206): the Lady Margaret of course. The Signallers alert the Corfe Garrison, and Eleanor is rescued and the Provost hanged. Then Henry of Rye and Deal, the Pope's lieutenant in England, arrives with a large force to demand her surrender; Eleanor simply pulls the firing lanyard of the big cannon known as Growler, taking both of Henry's feet off at the ankles and causing devastation among his troops. A siege ensues.

Sir John, the Fairy seneschal, has a secret radio and is able to keep Eleanor informed of the spreading insurrection: "Bodiam has declared for the King, Caernarvon has burned its charter. And Colchester, Warwick, Framlingham; Bramber, Cardiff, Chepstow" (216). It is interesting that in this list of places, all are familiar to us; there are none of the Latin names so persistent throughout the rest of the book. Even the Dubris we have encountered before in "Brother John" is here rendered as Dover. Among other things, this is a revolution in language. Sir John also tells Eleanor stories of "the times before there were castles on our hilltops and before the world knew anything of churches" (202/3), stories with a whiff of the vision Rafe had from the Fairy. And when they are awaiting the siege, John talks to her of "all subjects from gods to kings; of the land, its history and its people" (212) which again echoes the visions of both Rafe and Brother John.

When Sir John sees the signal from Henry demanding surrender he thinks: "This was the thing that had been ordained a thousand years; an era was about to come to an end" (183). Other than yet another hint of circularity (there are many throughout the story) it is not at all clear what is meant by this. By the end of the story Eleanor has been forced to surrender. There is a trial, of sorts, the sentence is commuted by the King, and she is imprisoned in the White Tower of the Tower of London for many years, while all the castles are brought down. Eventually, the King arranges for her to escape. She returns to Corfe, where John Faulkner is the only one to recognise her. There, years later, two furtive men arrive to assassinate her. She dies within sight of Corfe Castle. An era has not ended, and we only learn what John's comment means, that Eleanor's rebellion was the harbinger of change, in the "Coda".

The publishing history of the Coda is probably more complex than anything else in *Pavane*. In the magazine version, elements of what would become the Coda form an integral part of "Corfe Gate"; in the book it is separated out as an addendum to that story. In the light of this radical rewriting, there are differences between "Corfe Gate" as it appeared in the magazine and as it appeared in the book, but these differences are nowhere near as great as what went to make the Coda.

For a start, the "Coda" in the book is set an unspecified number of years after the last measure of the dance, but within a generation, the central figure is implicitly the son of Eleanor and Sir John; in the magazine, the interpolations that would later be extracted and revised to form the Coda are set in the twenty-second century. And in the magazine, this part of the story is told in first person by someone who introduces himself as "the son of a gentleman of the Privy Chamber" (Roberts 1966: 18), a position that suggests social change has been slower and less comprehensive than is implied in the book. (His costume, "a summer leotard of nylon lace and a cloak of Tyrian red" (Roberts 1966: 18) indicates how uncomfortable Roberts was trying to portray the distant future; in the book the timeline never gets more than a few decades after the now in which the author is writing; costumes do not need to be described because they are what his readers would have been wearing.) The visitor, Paul, is not a son of John the Seneschal, but during his visit to the ruins of Corfe he encounters a strange man, by implication a Fairy, who goes on to tell him the story of Eleanor's revolt. This recounting takes the form of what would be the book version of "Corfe Gate".

The letter from John Faulkner that points to the twentieth-century horrors of the Church avoided by slowing down progress (see below) does not appear in this version. Instead, the strange man refers to "the thing that appalled the Church a thousand years before Eleanor was born" (Roberts 1966: 62). This still presents the Church as doing bad things for good reasons, but it fits more comfortably into an alternate history reading than a cyclic history. But, confusingly, the strange man also insists that "[t]he Popes knew, as the Old Ones knew, that ... once, beyond our Time, there was a great civilisation" (Roberts 1966: 62). The dread carried over from this earlier civilisation is linked to nuclear power, a source of dread in much of Roberts's writing, from *The Furies* to *Kiteworld* and beyond, and which gives an added potency to the fission and fusion character of the Fairy symbol. The change from alternate history to cyclic history, therefore, seems to be less a case of Roberts switching boats in midstream, as him finally resolving a confusion.

Meanwhile, in the book version of *Pavane*, the separate "Coda" begins when a man arrives "on the hoverferry from Bourne Mouth" (230) and shortly thereafter catches a glimpse of Poole Power Station. This is clearly a different world, for the Church would never have sanctioned such technology. The man, another John (after Sir John and Brother John and Pope John), climbs to the ruins of Corfe Castle where he finds scratched on the walls a design featuring two arrows pointing inward and two pointing out, and this symbolises "the end of all Progress" (233), as the Fairies knew when they carved the symbol centuries before, a depiction of fission and fusion. We have seen this symbol a few times already in the book always associated with the Fairies.

John now opens and reads a letter from Sir John the seneschal, which tells us that here, in Corfe, "began that strange Revolt of the Castles; and here … began the freedom of the world" (233). Within ten years of the destruction of Corfe (a much shorter timescale than that given in the magazine version) the New World colonies broke free from Rome, and in their wake uprisings began across Europe and Australasia, and King Charles took his chance to secede from the Church. In an account that seems to combine the visions of Rafe and of Brother John, the letter goes on to lift a passage directly from the magazine version and say that "once, beyond our Time, beyond all the memories of men, there was a great civilization" (234), but a civilisation that tore itself apart. The Church knew it could not halt Progress, but slowing it, even by just half a century, it would give people "time to reach a little higher towards true Reason" (234). This was a priceless gift because "there was no Belsen. No Buchenwald. No Passchendaele" (234). Though if such things never happened, these names would have been meaningless. And the reason the world has climbed so rapidly from feudalism to democracy is because as soon as the Church saw her empire crumbling, she released all the knowledge she had been keeping in trust.

The revelation that the Church was aware of our history and had consciously acted to suppress it is nonsense, of course, since it "defies the logic of alternate history which requires that for a timeline to exist, all others must be snuffed out" (Clarke: 219). True, which is why, belatedly and not totally convincingly, Roberts claims he switched the character of the novel from alternate history to cyclic history. Hence, "When theorists come to taxonomize the exact interrelationship between counterfactual history and multiversal narratives, *Pavane* will be one of the more problematic texts to locate" (Clarke: 219). Nicholas Ruddick suggests another reading of Roberts's use of cyclic time, saying that it "provocatively challenges the linear temporality of the Judeo-Christian tradition ... [while also tending] ... to come into conflict with the linearity of traditional narrative itself" (Ruddick 1989a: 40). Personally I feel this is reading too much into the structure of the work, though I am rather more inclined to go along with Ruddick when he expands on this to suggest that *Pavane*, along with the similarly structured *The Chalk Giants* and *Kiteworld*, demonstrates "a willingness to challenge the most elementary assumptions of the reader concerning the nature of time, history, and the proper shape of narrative" (Ruddick 1989a: 40).

But the switch to cyclic history, and the explanation of that within the Coda, is not Roberts writing within the story, but writing out from it, directly addressing his late twentieth-century readers. As if he was acutely conscious of having made the Catholic Church the villain of the piece and was here trying to ameliorate the hurt, turn the villain into something approximating a hero. Of course it doesn't work, either in its own right or within the context of the novel as a whole. We have already seen in "The White Boat", that Church restrictions on technology seem to operate differently in different places, that England is somehow held back more than elsewhere. In such a context the unholy litany of Belsen, Buchenwald, Passchendaele sounds somewhat hollow. *Pavane* may have started as cyclic history but works better when read as alternate history. Either way, if Ruddick is right that the flaw lies here, it is not a fatal flaw, because the "Coda" is vital in providing a conclusion to the sequence that the death of Eleanor at the end of "Corfe Gate" cannot, on its own, convey.

BIBLIOGRAPHY

KEITH ROBERTS

"Corfe Gate" (Original Version). 1966. *Impulse* Vol. 1, Issue 5: 7–68.
Kiteworld. 1985. London: Gollancz.
Pavane. 1968 [1985]. London: Penguin.
"The Chalk Giant: Reflections by Keith Roberts". 1986. *Vector* 132 (June/ July): 6–8.
The Chalk Giants. 1974. London: Hutchinson.
The Furies. 1966. London: Rupert Hart-Davis.
The Grain Kings. 1976. London: Hutchinson.

Secondary Sources

Allan, Nina. 2018. The Fourfold Library (8): Keith Roberts, *Pavane*. *Foundation* 131: 69–71.

Clarke, Jim. 2019. *Science Fiction and Catholicism: The Rise and Fall of the Robot Papacy*. Canterbury: Gylphi.

Davidson, H.R. Ellis. 1964 [1975]. *Gods and Myths of Northern Europe*. Harmondsworth: Penguin.

Jordan, Michael. 1992 [1995]. *The Encyclopedia of Gods*. London: Kyle Cathie.

Kincaid, Paul. 1982. Of Men and Machines: Keith Roberts Interviewed. *Vector* 108 (June): 6–12.

———. 1986. A Mosaic of Words. *Vector* 132 (June/July): 2–5.

Ruddick, Nicholas. 1989a. Flaws in the Timestream: Unity and Disunity in Keith Roberts's Story-Cycles. *Foundation* 45 (Spring): 38–49.

———. 1989b. Flaws in the Timestream: Unity and Disunity in Keith Roberts's Story-Cycles: Part Two. *Foundation* 46 (Autumn): 14–26.

———. 1990. Flaws in the Timestream: Unity and Disunity in Keith Roberts's Story-Cycles (Conclusion). *Foundation* 47 (Winter): 33–42.

Suvin, Darko. 1983. Victorian Science Fiction, 1871–85: The Rise of the Alternative History Sub-Genre. *Science Fiction Studies* 10 (Part 2): 148–169.

CHAPTER 3

Future Historic

Abstract This chapter examines how Roberts uses the past as a setting for his near-future, what Brian Aldiss refers to as "future-historic". It gives a particular and distinctive voice to his science fiction, a voice that seems to owe more to Hardy and Kipling than it does to contemporary sf. Two aspects of his work in particular come to the fore in examining this voice: the socio-political, looking at the conservative impulse behind his work; and the technological, looking at the part that low-key, small-scale engineering contributes to his view of the world.

Keywords Rudyard Kipling • Conservatism • Semaphore • Steam engines

To understand why Keith Roberts features in so few general histories of science fiction, we might perhaps turn to the last such history that did draw attention to his work. In *Trillion Year Spree* (1986), Brian Aldiss writing with David Wingrove notes that Roberts "aspires towards that conservative tense: future-historic" (Aldiss: 479). In other words, although the world set out in *Pavane*, and in later key works such as *The Chalk Giants* (1974), *Molly Zero* (1980), and *Kiteworld* (1985), among others, is nominally the future, what we see of it is redolent of the past. In doing so, Roberts sets himself in opposition to how science fiction commonly

P. Kincaid, *Keith Roberts's* Pavane, Palgrave Science Fiction and
Fantasy: A New Canon,
https://doi.org/10.1007/978-3-031-71567-9_3

perceives itself. There are other, particularly British, writers such as Richard Cowper, who write within the future historic, whose inspiration comes more from the depths of English literature than the glittering surfaces of American science fiction. They borrow from authors whose work resonates with the landscape of southern England, writers like Thomas Hardy, even though Roberts emphatically declares himself not a fan of Hardy—"an infuriating writer. Much of his output I find frankly turgid" (Roberts 1997: 23)—while at the same time betraying an intimate knowledge of the novels. Or, in Roberts's case, the writer he most consistently references is Rudyard Kipling. But this is no widely recognised movement within the genre, and as such it is difficult to see where this work belongs within the broad picture. Thus, although acclaimed British writers such as Christopher Priest, M. John Harrison, Nina Allan, and Dave Hutchinson have acknowledged his influence; although Algis Budrys would declare unequivocally, "Keith Roberts is the best English SF writer" (Budrys 2012: 99); although Kingsley Amis would specifically reference *Pavane* in his own alternate history about a Catholic Church triumphant, *The Alteration* (1976), "to the world at large he was a secret" (Goddard: 68).

The work that first and most vividly deploys the future historic voice is *Pavane*, and to appreciate the part it plays in shaping the unique characteristics of that story cycle, it is necessary to consider two elements of the work: the socio-political and the technological.

Roberts is generally seen as being on the right politically. A view that became fixed after his late 1970s collection, *Ladies From Hell* (1979), which included some very clumsy contemporary references. In one story, "The Shack at Great Cross Halt", attackers cry out "Reach, by Huskalon! Reach, by Mikalfot!" (Roberts 1979: 83) a reference to a trade union leader and a left-wing politician who was later leader of the parliamentary Labour Party, both "excoriated by the Tory press in the 1970s as being bent upon the destruction of civilized values" (Kincaid 2001: 20). Such references led the critic Roz Kaveney to characterise him as "neoconservative", though she did concede that "the silliness of Roberts' views is surpassed by the power and beauty of his writing" (Kaveney: 24).

In fact, trying to maintain a political perspective on Roberts's work is not so straightforward as this might suggest. In one of the few overt political statements he allowed himself to make, for instance, he declared: "It seems to be obvious that in terms of both logic and morality, the only acceptable social order is communism" (Roberts 1986: 8). But this is not anything that comes across in his fiction, where the primary concern (in a way that echoes Hardy for instance) seems to be with a sort of social morality rather than any political formulation: "I have no politics, any more than I have a fixed religious faith; I simply feel that people should be treated as human beings" (Roberts 1986: 8). But his stories about the individual crushed by some monumental establishment are not as apolitical as he liked to pretend, and if not large-C Conservative, he was certainly conservative with a small "c". He interprets this small-c, non-political stance as being a moral stance, his stories repeatedly come around to the question of how to be a small, lonely individual in a big, impersonal world. And very often the only possible answer is that simply being in the world means taking responsibility for it. In a late story, "Kaeti and the Shadows", when Kaeti encounters the shadows of the victims of Hiroshima burnt into the buildings, the shadows tell her she is not to blame, but she can only reply, "I am. ... We all are" (Roberts 1992: 40). In Roberts, therefore, time and again we see that the choices his characters must make are both moral and political at the same time.

We need to pay attention to the moral uncertainty that taints so many of his characters. They are not, usually, bad people, but neither are they good. And if they do good in the end (not always the case), it is as often as not because of circumstances rather than any sense of moral duty. Roberts himself probably wouldn't have seen it like this; he would have just said that's the way people are. But of course, that is a moral question in its own right. Because he saw this as just a natural part of any character, he never drew particular attention to their moral strengths or failures, and so critics haven't paid attention to it either. Certainly, I haven't before now. But the more I revisit the work the more I can't help seeing it everywhere. Jesse Strange recalls an occasion when, as a boy, he "opened up a four horse Roby traction with her cocks shut, let the condensed water in front of the piston knock the end out of the bore. His heart had broken with the cracking iron" (13). He is, in other words, more emotionally affected by the damage to an unnamed machine than he will be to the death of an old friend, someone he will kill in a brutal and premeditated way. These are not people without moral and emotional complications. Despite his distress, old Eli had still beaten Jesse with a studded belt, because it was imperative that he learn how to look after the great engines, and such a disaster had, of course, never happened again. These are hard men, for "The business hadn't been built on softness" (23). Old Eli had "worked his few men hard for the wages he paid, and got his money's worth out of them" (13) and when Jesse inherited the business he continued in the same vein, he "drove his hauliers, he drove his machines, but most of all he drove himself" (125). Yet these same Stranges take a stand against the autocratic rule of the Church, if only because Church-imposed restrictions threaten their ability to make money, and so they are on the heroic side in the struggle for freedom traced throughout *Pavane*. Or are they? Because the Guild of Mechanics is agitating for better working conditions, and we learn that "the Church openly back[ed] the clamour of the Guilds for shorter hours and higher pay" (14), so in one thing at least the Church is seen to be socially liberal.

Similar moral and political ambiguity runs through every other measure of this dance. Rafe comes from a relatively poor family. His father is an estate clerk whose wage barely supports his family, so it is necessary for them to grow most of their own food. Rafe's fascination with the signal station is therefore unwelcome since it takes him away from necessary chores. By the time he was ten he had "received as much formal education as a child of his class could expect" (63). This too is one of the economic effects of the Church restricting technological advance. At ten, therefore, Rafe's family decide to apprentice him to a local tailor, but Rafe declares that he wants to be a Signaller, a move that will enhance the family's prestige, but will have an unspoken effect on their income. Details such as this display an awareness of the cruelty that Church rule imposes upon the poor, and a distinct class tension underlying the dissent we see throughout the story sequence. The only way out for Rafe is to join the elite society of the Signallers, just as for Brother John, from a similarly poor background, the only way to follow his dream is to join another elite, the Church itself.

John is another morally compromised figure, because what releases the "heresy [that] burned somewhere in the heart of Brother John" (98) is his enjoyment of the feverish sketching of the tortures of the Inquisition. The rebellion that his heresy inspires results in similar cruelty by the authorities, "Informers flourished; cottages were burned, whole towns fined. Bodies swayed at crossroads" (107). But again, as with the Inquisition, John is more observer than active participant, as we see at the end when he is summoned to cure "by the laying on of hands" (110), a quarryman who has gone blind. John recognises that he cannot cure the man, and the next morning when, before first light, the quarryman rises, walks to the quarry, and starts to work all that John and the man's wife can do is watch and pray until he has worked himself to death. Like Kaeti with the Hiroshima shadows, they can do nothing but simply being in the world means taking responsibility for it.

Again, in "The White Boat", there is no clear-cut moral choice. The boat itself is engaged in criminal activity, smuggling, and the crew are not above discussing whether to kill Becky; yet they are the very image of freedom, the white that signifies good against the black of Becky's cruel daily world (remember, like Jesse, she is viciously beaten by her father). And Becky herself makes contradictory moral choices, first betraying the boat to the authorities then springing the trap so the boat can get away. "Physically, she has not escaped the black rock that has ground down her parents and everyone else in the village, but the boat has given her a dream of freedom, of being an individual away from the uniformity of village life, and that is enough" (Kincaid 2001: 23).

And so we come to the first and last of the measures, "Corfe Gate", the story that closes off the sequence and from which it all sprang. Here the focus is upon Lady Eleanor, an ambiguous figure, the first and only member of the aristocracy to hold centre stage. In herself she represents all the classes in this England: her grandmother was a barmaid who married into the middle class; her mother was a member of the rich Strange family, but a commoner who married into the aristocracy; while Eleanor herself is born into the aristocracy but would not, usually by reason of her sex, expect to inherit the position she occupies as castellan of Corfe.

There is an unquestioned conservative air to this situation. So far all the agitation and dissent has come from the lower classes from which Eleanor has escaped, but it takes a member of the aristocracy to actually launch the rebellion. And though the rebellion is triggered by Eleanor's concern that new Church levies will lead to starvation among her people in Dorset, this is far from being a communist revolution. In fact Eleanor is a royalist and nationalist who achieves what she does by proclaiming herself loyal to King Charles against a Church that she portrays as foreign interlopers: "I'm getting so tired of strangers lording it over England, even if it is heresy to say so" (197). Yet it is perhaps significant that each of the three central characters in this story cycle who move into a more elite circle—Rafe joining the Signallers, John joining the Church, and Eleanor in the aristocracy—must die in the end. Dissent is a moral duty but it comes at a cost.

One of the interesting features of the work is that this moral and political dissent that the work as a whole relates is almost entirely focussed upon technology. As Nicholas Ruddick puts it, the story cycle explores "the process whereby society emerges from feudalism into enlightenment, with science and technology as the agent of transformation" (Ruddick 1989:

15). This is, perhaps, overstating the case, yet it is inarguable that throughout *Pavane* technology is both the hinge around which change occurs, and at the same time a key signifier of the past.

Part of the reason I suspect that Roberts was uneasy with being classified as a science fiction writer was because he had little interest in science as a harbinger of the future, in the invention of strange devices. Rather, he is concerned with the technology that has got us to where we are now, that explains the modern world. There is an element of nostalgia about this. He makes a significant remark in his introduction to the story "The Scarlet Lady" (1966), one of so many early stories about cars: "There was a time when cars had faces. Now they're just tin boxes. Or maybe that's the child in me, remembering heightened favours" (Roberts 1989: 24). And when the narrator of "I Lose Medea" (1972) comes across "a vintage Morris motor-car" and says it "pleased me a lot because I like old machinery" (Roberts 1976: 198) you can hear Roberts himself speaking. The number of old, workaday engines and devices that fill his fiction is one sign of his small-c conservatism: "[T]he notion that the proper survival of the world depends upon the sorts of motors which can be repaired by an averagely skilled man with grease under his fingernails" (Kincaid 2001, 21).

Roberts's preference for low-key, practical, everyday technology rather than fancy devices, and the way this put him at odds with traditional views of science fiction, is illustrated in his memoir, *Lemady* (1997), when he insists that "an old witticism has it that certain of the American magazines had turned science fiction into a branch of *Popular Mechanics*. Maybe in my own small way, I was trying to do the same" (Roberts 1997: 70). He has said, in an interview with me, "I'm fascinated with machinery up to the level I can understand it" (Kincaid 1986: 5), and throughout his work there is an insistence on the understandability of technology. This approach to the machine is typified by an anecdote he told about writing *The Furies*. He wanted his protagonist at one point to drive a Saracen Armoured Personnel Carrier, but though he could find technical information about the vehicle, none of this told him what it was like to be in one. Then he met a member of the Territorial Army who had just been on manoeuvres in a Saracen. His wry description was "Poke your head in a dustbin ... and get somebody to bang the end with a sledgehammer" (Kincaid 1982: 9). Roberts was so taken with this description that he used it word for word in the novel.

So when, in a peculiarly ill-judged survey of Roberts's work, Bruce Gillespie says of *Pavane* that "Roberts invents and lovingly describes the

3 FUTURE HISTORIC   35

details of two complete alternative technologies" (Gillespie: 3), neither of the technologies he mentions, the steam engines and the semaphore stations, are inventions. In fact the way the Church slows down technological development actually returns it to a level that Roberts can understand. Thus, as I mentioned in Chap. 2, the Burrell engine comes from a famous maker of steam engines that survived into the 1920s and some of whose engines survive to this day. The Lady Margaret, with a load of 30 tonnes and managing up to 20 miles per hour on the open road, can be compared to the *Quo Vadis*, a typical Burrell road locomotive built in 1922: "8-nhp, double-crank compound, scenic-type showman's engine. ... Engines of this type frequently hauled loads of 50 tons or more hundreds of miles, averaging 12 miles an hour, as well as working generating equipment on arrival" (quoted, Kincaid 2014: 282). As for the network of semaphore stations, just such a network was established in 1795 during the Napoleonic Wars. Using these stations allowed a message to be sent between the Admiralty at Whitehall to Deal in Kent in sixty seconds. The system was retired in 1836 when superseded by the railway telegraph system, just as, in "Corfe Gate", we learn that the Signallers are using a new technology, the radio, which is not yet sanctioned by the Church.

Roberts practically never invented technology, even when the devices he describes seem outlandish. For instance, the kites that feature in *Kiteworld* are based on the manlifting kites devised by Samuel Cody before the First World War, only to be superseded almost before they were invented by the advent of hydrogen balloons (although in a 1986 interview Roberts insisted "The Cody system of strings are real, of course, and are still flown" (Kincaid 1986: 4)). Indeed much of the lovingly described technology that appears in *Pavane* is equipment that Roberts would himself have been familiar with. Thus, the close attention to mechanical details when he describes Brother John at work on his lithography—"Each bed was lifted to printing height by a tall lever and propelled by a hefty wooden-spoked wheel; over the bed an iron frame supported a leather-covered wedge, adjustable for pressure. A brass tympan, hinged at the farther end of the bed and tensioned by lead screws along its edges, protected the stone from the wedge" (88/9)—is probably based on the equipment he would have used as an art student. And the passing reference to "Senefelder's laundry list" (92) is a tip of the hat to Aloys Senefelder (1771–1834), who invented lithography when he jotted his laundry list down on limestone with a grease pencil and realised he could etch away the rest of the surface. While Roberts's father makes a brief appearance in

"Corfe Gate" when one of the entertainers who visits Lady Eleanor brings a strange device: "A strip of unknown substance was fed into it, a handle turned; a limelight spat and hissed, and pictures, flickering and seemingly alive, danced across a screen" (203). Indeed, given the way, in *Pavane* and in *The Chalk Giants*, the future rolls around in a great circle, I have mused on whether, in his father's projection booth, "seeing the reels being rewound and the same story being projected once more, [he found] a metaphor he would henceforth apply to history" (Kincaid 2001: 21).

In an interview, Roberts recounted how "John Brunner once challenged me … to explain why in all alternate history novels the state of technology is invariably inferior to ours. … [N]ow I'd probably answer in one word. Atavism" (Kincaid 1982: 10). Personally I don't think that is an answer to the question. In *Pavane*, of course, the whole point of the novel is that technological advance has been very deliberately retarded. But Roberts also has always had what we might almost call a romantic attachment to old-fashioned technology; there is a human connection to the machine that he regards with far more affection than more impersonal technology. There is a human scale to the devices we encounter, a tactile quality, as when Jesse cuts the speed of the *Lady Margaret* and "felt through his boot soles the slackening pull on the drawbar" (16). This level of technology is something directly felt, made more real because it is tangible, and because of that the machines connect directly with the characters and therefore carry a moral weight. Technology is integral to the moral decisions that convey the socio-political pulse of the novel as discussed above.

Thus, time and again, the beginning of dissent from the rule of the Church is tied to the desire for some technological change. Eli Strange wants to fit the modern and more efficient oil burners that are available for the road trains, but they have not been blessed by the Church. Brother John is first identified as an irritant, a possible troublemaker, when he uses mineral grease on his printing press instead of the stinking bear grease. And Eleanor "remembered from her schooling that a wire suitably wound on an earthenware former, could be made to glow redly if sufficient difference in potential could be created between its ends" (194), and hence has electric light and heating installed in Corfe Castle, though the Church has resolutely refused to sanction the use of electricity for domestic use. Technology is simply a way to make everyday life a little easier, but the steadfast refusal of the Church to allow such improvements comes more and more to feel like a direct attack upon ordinary people, and thus rebellion grows.

This revolt therefore takes the form of a conflict between new and old, between the future and the historic. One illustration of this is something that would have been close to the heart of Keith Roberts, with his sporty, open-topped Triumph Spitfire: the Papal Bull, *Petroleum Veto*, which limited the capacity of internal combustion engines to 150cc. The wealthy owners of petrol vehicles, therefore, had been forced to fit gaudy sails to help move them along, hence the nickname "butterfly cars" (16). The image of the modern world being held in check by the past is perfectly captured in the opening sentences of "Corfe Gate": "The column of horsemen trotted briskly, harness jangling, making no attempt to keep to the side of the road. Behind the soldiers the tourist cars of the wealthy bunched and jostled, motors sputtering" (177). The modern world may be restless and impatient, but the more the Church tries to keep it bottled up, the more likely it is to burst forth.

This very issue, of course, presents another problem with reading the book as a cyclic rather than an alternate history. As L.J. Hurst puts it: it is a simple question of resources: "[H]ow much oil would be available to a feudal economy, that would necessitate the Papal Bull 'Petroleum Veto'?" (Hurst: 19). This is not just a question of where and how does the society of the novel extract and refine and distribute oil (though we get no glimpse of such an infrastructure within the story cycle); but more pertinently, we know that our own society has used up most of the oil and the coal produced by millennia of slow geological processes, so if this is a successor society to our own, how have these scarce resources been renewed? It would require a stretch of time that belies the notion that the Catholic Church might somehow remember the follies of our own prior age. Though, of course, if we are seeing an alternate history rather than a cyclic history, then the notion of remembering a previous age is also negated. Roberts had a matter-of-fact response to such nit-picking, however. Challenged on how Lady Eleanor could wear patterned nylons when there is no evidence of an advanced petro-chemical industry in the book, Roberts replied, "[I]t puzzled me as well, but since nylons are mentioned they must have had one, mustn't they?" (Roberts 1986: 7).

BIBLIOGRAPHY

KEITH ROBERTS

Kaeti On Tour. 1992. Feltham: Sirius Book Company.
Kiteworld. 1985. London: Gollancz.
Ladies from Hell. 1979. London: Gollancz.
Lemady: Episodes of a Writer's Life. 1997. Gillette, NJ: Wildside Press.
Molly Zero. 1980. London: Gollancz.
Pavane. 1968 [1985]. London: Penguin.
"The Chalk Giant: Reflections by Keith Roberts". 1986. *Vector* 132 (June/July): 6–8.
The Chalk Giants. 1974. London: Hutchinson.
The Furies. 1966. London: Rupert Hart-Davis.
The Grain Kings. 1976. London: Hutchinson.
Winterwood and Other Hauntings. 1989. Scotforth, Lancs: Morrigan.

SECONDARY SOURCES

Aldiss, Brian with David Wingrove. 1986 [1988]. *Trillion Year Spree*. London: Paladin.
Budrys, Algis. 2012. *Benchmarks Continued: F&SF 'Books' Columns 1975–1982*. Ansible ed. Reading.
Gillespie, Bruce. 1994. The Not-Quite Career of Keith Roberts. *Scratch Pad* 14 (December): 1–7.
Goddard, Jim. 2000. Keith Roberts: A Remembrance. *Locus* 478 (November): 68.
Hurst, L.J. 1985. A Timeless Dance: Keith Roberts' *Pavane* Re-examined. *Vector* 124/125 (April–May): 17–19.
Kaveney, Roz. 1981. Science Fiction in the 1970s: Some Dominant Themes and Personalities. *Foundation* 22 (June): 5–35.
Kincaid, Paul. 1982. Of Men and Machines: Keith Roberts interviewed. *Vector* 108 (June): 6–12.
———. 1986. A Mosaic of Words. *Vector* 132 (June/July): 2–5.
———. 2001. Future Historical: The Fiction of Keith Roberts. *Steam Engine Time* 3 (December): 20–24.
———. 2014. Pavane. In *Call and Response*, 278–299. Harold Wood: Beccon Publications.
Ruddick, Nicholas. 1989. Flaws in the Timestream: Unity and Disunity in Keith Roberts's Story-Cycles: Part Two. *Foundation* 46 (Autumn): 14–26.

CHAPTER 4

Pharisees and Inquisitors

Abstract One of the fundamental elements in the world of *Pavane*, an inescapable feature that has to be central to any evaluation of the book, is the role of religion. This is not just the fact that the Catholic Church plays the part of the villain in this story, something that Roberts would later come to regret, but ranged against the Church and the social and economic system it has created, are other belief systems. The dissent that runs throughout the story cycle is intimately connected to an unlikely alliance of other belief systems. Anglicanism survives as an underground movement, but here it works in concert with folk beliefs, with the Fairies, and with a survival of Norse mythology. This chapter examines how the interplay of these competing belief systems is essential to the structure of the story and any interpretation of what happens.

Keywords Catholic Church • Anglicanism • Fairies • Norse myth

Keith Roberts insisted that *Pavane* returns again and again "to the theme of unquestioning and excessive loyalty" (Kincaid 1982: 10). It is possible to make that case. We might look, for example, at the family loyalty of the Strange family, at the demands placed on its members by the Guild of Signallers, at the loyalty that Lady Eleanor feels towards the ordinary

P. Kincaid, *Keith Roberts's* Pavane, Palgrave Science Fiction and Fantasy: A New Canon,
https://doi.org/10.1007/978-3-031-71567-9_4

people in her demesne, and above all at the unquestioned loyalty insisted upon by the all-powerful Church. Yet this loyalty rarely is unquestioned, and what we see within the various stories is more often betrayal than loyalty.

In the end, however much we might strain our interpretation to arrive at such a reading, we are forced to conclude, as Nicholas Ruddick points out, that "loyalty is not the unifying subject or theme of *Pavane*" (Ruddick 1989: 47). Rather, it is a sequence of stories about the combination of influences that make us stand up for something, and so how dissent develops and grows into open rebellion.

What prompts these characters to take their stand, what unifies these various influences, is belief. *Pavane* is a cycle of stories that, collectively, explore the question of belief, that consider the secular effect that belief has upon progress, technology, society. But to airily talk of belief in this way, as though it were some simple, uniform thing, a single straight line that can be traced through each of the stories, is to comprehensively misunderstand the book. The universe of belief presented within *Pavane* is far and away the most complex aspect of the whole work. Yes, it seems simple: the Catholic Church has triumphed, and what we are presented with is a world in which everything is shaped by the autocratic dictates coming from Rome. What drives the plot is ever-widening dissatisfaction with the everyday effect of these rulings: a simple, uni-directional story with a clear villain.

But that is not really how it is: the Catholic Church is under siege the whole time; it faces a host of enemies operating under the radar throughout the country, forces that foment, encourage, and exploit the dissatisfactions that will eventually end Catholic rule. Some of these are secular: the rise of a powerful commercial class, the king; but most of them are tied to rival belief systems. There is the cult of Balder, a derivation from Norse mythology that acts as a rival interpretation of the story of Christ; there are the Fairies, an underground that operates in plain sight, and whose very existence suggests that the Catholic Church does not control the religious landscape; and there is the survival of Protestantism, supposedly destroyed forever by the Armada but still very much alive among the people of England. The way that the religious and the secular inform each other, and the interaction of the different belief systems, is what makes *Pavane* such a rich and rewarding landscape to explore.

The immediate question to be considered in any examination of this book, of course, is whether *Pavane* is anti-Catholic. We must, from the start, acknowledge that the Coda tells us that from an historical perspective the rule of the Church is seen to be beneficial, that, as Zachary Leader says of Kingsley Amis's near-mirror of *Pavane*, *The Alteration*, "[t]he uninterrupted reign of the Catholic Church means no democracy, no nationalism, no socialism, no national socialism" (quoted, Clarke: 234). Presumably with this in mind, in his 1969 review of *Pavane*, M. John Harrison averred that Roberts managed "to treat both sides of the argument with their due sympathy" (Bould & Reid: 53), thus detecting an even-handedness in the treatment of Catholicism that Roberts himself suspected wasn't there. While Roberts insisted that for all it might give shelter to those who commit evil, the Church in itself wasn't evil; nevertheless, he would always feel that he had made the Church into a villain, something he would try to repair in later works such as *The Chalk Giants* and *Kiteworld*. However, Roberts's argument that the Church is not evil isn't entirely borne out by his describing his Church as modelled on the setup at about the time of Innocent VIII, pope from 1484 to 1492, and referencing the *Malleus Maleficarum*, and the appointment of Torquemada as the head of the Inquisition in Spain.

In his study of Catholicism in science fiction, Jim Clarke argues that the very structure of *Pavane* as an alternate history marks it out as "yet another milestone in the lengthy lineage of anti-Catholicism in British letters" (Clarke, 204). One of the disadvantages of alternate histories, as Clarke points out, is that they tend to assume that history is frozen at a certain point, that one key event will change the world irrevocably. That doesn't take account of sociological changes. The assassination of Hitler would not necessarily have had much effect: the Versailles settlement, the economic collapse of 1929, and the rise of right-wing nationalist parties across Europe are likely to have given rise to something similar to Nazism in Germany even without the personal charisma of Hitler. But though Roberts points to the assassination of Elizabeth as the key moment in the ascent of Catholicism, he is careful to suggest that this is part of a wider story: the success of the Armada leading to the imposition of Catholic rule, and the fact that Britain, which in our history tended to stay out of European religious conflicts throughout the seventeenth century, is now available to make a decisive intervention in what was in reality a very finely balanced conflict between Protestant nations and Catholic. As the historian, Paul Hazard, points out, within a century of the Armada, even in our history, Protestantism throughout Europe was on the back foot and the Catholic powers were looking forward to their approaching and total victory. Nevertheless, as Randall Collins says: "The notion that victory over Protestantism would have established a uniform and unshakeable Catholic despotism throughout Europe ... runs contrary to a long-term pattern" (quoted, Clarke: 206–7). Iain Rowan picks up on this to suggest that this continued dominance by the Church is a flaw in the structure: "From the late medieval period onwards the Church never possessed the stability that Roberts portrays it as having across the next four hundred years, and it is a stretch to imagine that any such hegemony could have persisted for quite so long, in such a stable form" (Rowan: np). But in *Pavane* the regime is not "unshakeable"; it is being tested at every point of the novel. Furthermore, we know that secular regimes tended to use people educated in and by the Church for administration of the state (Cardinal Wolsey and Thomas More in Britain only a generation before the reign of Elizabeth), and from writers like John Banville we know that even without such administrators the Catholic Church retained a stranglehold on social policy in Ireland right into the 1960s and beyond, exactly the sort of influence pictured in *Pavane*. In truth therefore, while we might accept that the Church never achieved the level of despotism portrayed within the book, nevertheless it did aspire to such control. And the narrative function that the Church plays within *Pavane* is not a totally unfair picture.

But then, the role that the Catholic Church plays here is not meant to be seen in isolation, but rather stands in contrast to what might have been under Protestantism. The underlying notion, that the supremacy of the Catholic Church has retarded social and technological development, has refused to "release scientific knowledge until men were ready for it" (Ruddick 1989: 41) is a literalisation of the old notion of the Protestant work ethic. The idea of the protestant work ethic and its link to capitalism was first proposed by the German sociologist, Max Weber, in *The Protestant Ethic and the Spirit of Capitalism* (1904). The idea was further developed and popularised by the Christian Socialist, R.H. Tawney, in his classic work *Religion and the Rise of Capitalism* (1926) which argued that the Protestant Reformation led to a division between commerce and social morality, and thus subordinated Christian teaching to the pursuit of wealth. As the historian Diarmaid MacCulloch has pointed out, "Protestant England and the Protestant Netherlands undoubtedly both became major economic powers in the seventeenth and eighteenth centuries" though he goes on to say that "[a]ny simple link between religion and capitalism founders on both objections and counter-examples" (MacCulloch: 605).

Nevertheless, for most of the twentieth century Tawney's view gained more popular support than more nuanced historical perspectives, and both Tom Shippey and L.J. Hurst point out Tawney's influence on *Pavane*. The common view is that during the religious wars of the sixteenth and seventeenth centuries, the Catholic Church would persecute Galileo, insist that there could be no other inhabited worlds since Jesus Christ only appeared in our world, and otherwise limit the scope of scientific creativity through a variety of papal bulls and an insistent social conservatism. In contrast the Protestant nations enabled the democratisation of religious observance, allowing the Bible to be published in the vernacular which meant that people no longer had to rely on a priestly elite to translate and interpret the laws of God. Since ordinary people now had a direct relationship with God, the leaders of various strict Protestant sects promoted the idea of hard work and contributing to the wealth of the world as a way of earning divine favour. In this way, Protestantism "helped justify industrial and monetary progress and reorganisation" which Catholicism hindered: "The only major economic development that originated in Catholicism was double entry bookkeeping" (Hurst: 18). This fostered a spirit of individualism and enquiry which in turn led to scientific discoveries and technological inventions unhindered by papal diktat, and so the Industrial Revolution which first began to develop in the seventeenth century and gathered pace over the next two hundred years was born in the Protestant world. This version of history, which reduced to basics implies that the Reformation fostered the Industrial Revolution, a notion condemned by Max Weber as a "foolish and doctrinaire thesis" (quoted Ruddick 1989: 41), isn't quite accurate, the Catholic Church particularly in France and Italy would itself sponsor valuable scientific work, and many of the philosophers whose ideas underlay much of the scientific endeavour of the Reformation were themselves Catholic. But as Tawney says, "Systems prepare their own overthrow by a preliminary process of petrifaction" (Tawney: 75), and by the time of the religious wars the rule of the Catholic Church across Europe had petrified. *Pavane* paints a picture of such petrifaction extended by the simple expedient of nipping any challenge to the system in the bud; but still the delayed overthrow was to come, and the novel examines the way different classes and levels of society begin to react against the petrifaction.

A simplistic view would have it that *Pavane* presents a world in which the counter-Reformation enjoyed complete success and wiped out the Protestant heresy in England. This idea just doesn't work. The Catholic

Church had been opposed by the proto-Protestant Lollards more than a century before Elizabeth I came to the throne; the Reformation itself can be dated to the moment that Martin Luther nailed his Ninety-Five Theses to the door of All Saints' Church at Wittenberg in October 1517; and it was established in England when Henry VIII was proclaimed Head of the Church in England in 1531. Although Protestants in England were persecuted during the reign of Mary I, Protestantism was well established by the time Elizabeth came to the throne in 1558, and by the time of her assassination 30 years later, Protestantism had been the religion of a substantial proportion of the population for over 50 years. This was not a new and fragile challenge to the Catholic authorities, and just as in our world, Catholicism went underground during the religious persecutions of the sixteenth and seventeenth centuries, only to re-emerge later, so in this world Protestantism goes underground but "remains as one of the many stories that survive in England" (Bilson: 59). There are numerous signs of this survival. Bilson notes, for instance, that "[t]he Stranges give their children the names of Old Testament patriarchs (Eli, Jesse) and strong old queens of England (Margaret, Eleanor) rather than the names of saints" (Bilson: 50). And when Rafe graduates from the College of Signals he is required to spend a full day in the physically arduous task of transmitting "in plaintalk the entire of the Book of Nehemiah" (68). Until the middle of the sixteenth century, this was always known as the Second Book of Ezra, but at that time Protestant Bibles produced in Geneva began to refer to it as the Book of Nehemiah. This was a continuing difference between Protestant and Catholic Bibles until long enough after the historical turning point to suggest that the Guild of Signallers is, secretly, a Protestant body. It is only later, in "Brother John", that there is a specific reference to the "resurging power of Anglicanism" (103) as an ideal vehicle for the new dissent.

If Protestantism represents, as the historian Paul Hazard put it, "a revolt of the individual conscience against the intrusion of authority in matters of faith" (Hazard: 94), then *Pavane* catalogues the nature and progress of such a revolt. It is a world about to be shaped by a form of Protestantism, as, in turn, the rebellions of Jesse, John, and Becky are guided by an individual conscience shaped by a mixture of faith, aspiration, and desire. But this is not a form of Protestantism that we might recognise. Although, as I show above, it is unlikely that the Protestant faith would have been entirely eliminated by the victory of the Catholic Church, the version of it that would begin to re-emerge in the late twentieth century of the novel is shaped by a range of other influences ranging from ancient gods to modern capitalism. One of the effects of Protestantism, as Paul Hazard put it, was that "authority is respected no longer" (Hazard: 97). As people begin to chafe against "the old cry of the Church, to submit and to adore" (103), so the reversion of the Anglican Community, particularly its renewed association with old ways, makes it an ideal vehicle for this new dissent. Religious dissent is therefore equated with political dissent, and that is what we see throughout *Pavane*, our protagonists in each measure are, in often small and personal ways, dissenting and that dissent builds into a threat to the whole structure of religious authority in the country.

But this dissent is not purely Anglican in origin or in character, because the Protestantism that emerges during the course of the story cycle is intimately connected with other, older religious systems. There are folk beliefs such as the pagan, or certainly non-Catholic, practices among the country folk that Margaret is aware of, the "furrows where bread and other things were buried in defiance of Mother Church" and "the balefires on the mounds of the dead where the Old Ones watched for a time" (123). As a Strange, we can presume that Margaret at least inclines towards Protestantism. As most who do not follow the established religion probably do in such circumstances, she makes a show of faith but does not join the priest at prayer and "held her tongue at confession" (122). So, the awareness of, and sympathy for, such folk practices is not seen as incompatible with Anglicanism. Indeed, the dissent that Margaret and her daughter, Eleanor, will be associated with emerges from a combination of the Protestant work ethic she has imbibed as a member of the commercial class, and the folk beliefs that are followed by the people around her. Jim Clarke would argue that, as the target of this dissent, the Church is "not merely the progenitor of an anti-scientific dystopia. It is also the suppressor of something older and chthonic, signified in part by Nordic myth" (Clarke: 218). Yet these suppressed folk beliefs, partly derived from Norse myth as represented by the Christ-like sacrifice of Balder recounted in Rafe's vision, are not necessarily hostile to the Catholic Church. As the Old One says to Margaret: "Do not despise your Church; for she has a wisdom beyond your understanding. Do not despise her mummeries; they have a purpose that will be fulfilled" (147). This is not a simple battle between the Catholic Church on the one side, and an unlikely alliance of other belief systems on the other, the whole thing is a lot more subtle and complex than that.

And it is the Old Ones, the People of the Heath, the Fairies, that are at the heart of this complexity. As Judith Hanna points out, the presence of the fairies undermines "any attempt to explain the world of *Pavane* in rational and scientific terms" (Hanna: 11), but she goes on to insist that they are "not a whimsical flaw" but make a serious point about the world shown here. A seventeenth-century Puritan broadside ballad, "Farewell Rewards and Fairies", declares that

> fairies
> Were of the old profession;
> Their songs were Ave Maries,
> Their dances were procession. (quoted, Hanna: 11)

The "old profession" is Catholicism, and the Puritans were pointing out how right it was to be rid of them. Protestantism encouraged secularism, individual conscience given precedence over ritual, individual judgement replacing faith in higher powers. In the world of *Pavane*, therefore, a world in which Protestantism has not cast out the belief system symbolised by the fairies, "Fate is not random but purposeful; no sparrow falls but is part of [a] divine plan" (Hanna: 11). The fairies are equated not just with the old ways, given that the Fairy who treats Rafe with basic country medicine also invokes the Norns and Yggdrasil, but also with the universe of belief associated with Catholicism. Thus, before his injuries Rafe, who, as a Signaller, is by implication inclined to Protestantism, doesn't believe in them. In his isolated post he is said to be in danger from "wolves and Fairies, though the former were virtually extinct in the south and he was young enough to laugh at the latter" (71). It is interesting that Rafe, a country boy who spends so much of his childhood around the stone circle and ancient barrows of Avebury and Silbury Hill, a landscape of mystery and wonder closely associated with the Fairies, should not himself believe in them. It suggests that either they do not associate much with ordinary mortals or they do not appear to be any different from other people. As far as most people are concerned, therefore, all that is known of them is rumour and folk tales, such as the suggestion that Brother John, being "in league with the People of the Heath, could be transported by magically swift means away from danger" (107). Nothing that we see of Brother John, of course, indicates that this might be the case.

There is nothing magical or supernatural about the Fairy who treats Rafe, but she does represent the survival of something, a belief system, a way of doing things, a measure of independence, that would have been destroyed had Protestantism and its associated rationalism been victorious; but at the same time their very invocation of old ways makes them antipathetic to the ruling Catholic Church. They bring visions of how things were and how they might be otherwise, they are associated with the antiquity of the land, and with ancient belief systems, and above all they hint at the cycle of the ages. In the final measure, "Corfe Gate", Eleanor's "deep connection with the guardian spirits of the land is manifested in her closeness to her Fairy seneschal, John Falconer" (Ruddick, 1989a: 46). It is Sir John who teaches Eleanor to drive, and who is seen operating the illicit radio, the intersection of old beliefs and modern technology that we see, for instance, in Becky's interaction with the white boat. It needs both, the old and the new, to finally arouse the sleeping giant that is Britain.

The appearance of the Fairies, their key role within the book, brings us to the writer who had a greater influence on Keith Roberts than any other, Rudyard Kipling, who, as Roberts said, "exploded on me at a very tender age" (Kincaid 1982: 8). It was Kipling, who, in *Puck of Pook's Hill* (1906), writes about the Dymchurch Flit, the departure of the Pharisees (Fairies) with the coming of the "Reformatories". But it is notably not Protestantism as such that drives the Fairies away, but rather the conflict engendered by the Reformation: "Goodwill among Flesh an' Blood is meat an' drink to 'em, an' ill-will is poison. ... This Reformatories tarrified the Pharisees same as the reaper goin' round a last stand o' wheat tarrifies rabbits" (Kipling: 210). The way that Kipling associates the Fairies with the smugglers of Romney Marsh raises the possibility that we might read the smugglers of the White Boat as yet another appearance of the Old Ones. There is nothing in the text itself to confirm such a reading, but it does at least fit with the underlying impression that anyone acting against the authority of the Church is to some extent in alliance with the Fairies.

The view expressed by Judith Hanna, that Catholicism enabled a climate of belief in the supernatural, while Protestantism encouraged a more secular individualism, which is why the Fairies have no place in a Protestant world except as icons to be destroyed, can therefore be no more that part of the picture, and a small part at that. If it was the full picture, the Fairies would play no part in the rise of a modernist revolt against Catholic authority. For a start, the only expressly supernatural aspect of the Fairies that we see comes at the end of "The Signaller", when the unnamed Fairy leads the spirit of Rafe away from his dead body and into another realm. Other than that, the Fairies we do encounter, most notably John the

Seneschal, seem little different from ordinary mortals in their behaviour, their position, or their use of technology. Nevertheless, Hanna is right to say that the Fairies undermine a purely rational interpretation of *Pavane*, but rather that they are a demonstration of the way that this world and all that occurs within it, both in the imposition of authority and in the revolt against that authority, is indelibly shaped by a belief system which must be understood if we are to understand the world. "The Fairies are our passport into the other time, whether alternate history or cyclic, in which *Pavane* exists" (Kincaid 2014: 286).

Belief, which is, of course, central to defining the interplay between the different groups that interact throughout the story cycle, isn't everything. The revolt we witness throughout the novel is primarily against the temporal power of the Church, the resistance to technology, to social advance. We see that in the commercial role of the Strange family, in the role of King Charles, and in the way that Eleanor begins her rebellion in a dispute over taxes. But the spiritual power of the Church is inevitably and inextricably mixed up with this. Brother John's feverish sketching of the grim work of the Inquisition taught him that the Church's concern for souls is at the expense of broken bodies and thus, as he sees it, "His drink is blood, His food is flesh. His sacraments work and misery and endless hopeless pain" (113). As well as looking forward to the blind quarryman who works himself to death prompting John's final vision, this resonates with a similarly bloody image in Rafe's final vision, but one that plays out to very different effect. Rafe sees Balder, who is not the Christos of Mother Church but must play the same role, killed upon the tree Yggdrasil, and "from His blood sprang warmth again and grass and sunlight, the meadow flowers and the calling, mating birds" (79). The old ways see blood as integral to growth and renewal, but when the Church does come along at last, claiming for their own Christos all that was true of Balder, it is accompanied by wars and bloodshed. The mirrored visions of Rafe and John relate to the way the spiritual power of the Church has real-world, temporal, and cruel consequences, thus illustrating why it demands opposition. The Church taught John to find God in himself, and when he witnessed the tortures of the Inquisition, he saw the pain and cruelty in himself. As he wanders thereafter, he encounters disease and suffering and hunger, and this is the world that God made. In the face of all that, John can only revolt against God. Similarly, when Margaret watches the priest deliver the last rites to old Jesse Strange, she wonders: "This God they prattle on about, where's His justice, where's His compassion? … is He satisfied when men drop dead chopping stone out for his temples" (145), that last a clear reference to the circumstances of John's final vision. And when Margaret looks for an alternative, she turns to "the wind … the heaths and the old grey hills" (145). In other words, the old ways, the old gods, who are part and parcel of the landscape.

The way the secular and temporal, politics and belief all intermingle in the growth of revolution is made explicit at the end. When Eleanor begins her rebellion, practically her first act is to expel the priest, Father Sebastian. "I said I knew I was damned because I'd damned myself. I didn't have to wait for any god to do it for me." She continues: "I just wasn't a Christian any more" (211). Her disavowal of organised religion in this confession to the Fairy John Faulkner is an appeal for alliance with the Old Ones. As John says, when Eleanor is excommunicated, their people will disavow Rome. And the seneschal thinks "The old thoughts, the first thoughts of the first people ever; for the seneschal was of the ancient kind" (215). Her repudiation of the Church is complete when the two assassins arrive and she says: "[Y]our God is such an angry God, isn't he? Far angrier than mine" (224). Her rebellion is designed to espouse new technologies to advocate for a new, kinder social order but the only way forward to achieve these ends is to turn back to the old ways. But at the end she tells John: "The Old Way is dead" (225). As if, as in Kipling, the defeat of the Church means the end of the old ways too.

Though perhaps the death of the old way has been exaggerated; or perhaps, in keeping with the cyclic character of the work, the old way has died only to become the new way. For when, in the Coda, another John arrives at Corfe, he finds, carved on the wall of the ruined castle, the symbol of a "circle enclosing a crab-network of triangles and crossing lines", a symbol also displayed on the medallion he wears: "The symbol like a time-charm stirred depths of Self and memory" (231). It is a symbol we have glimpsed repeatedly throughout the various measures of this dance, depicting arrows pointing inward and out, fission and fusion, and it is an image indelibly associated with the Fairies. The rather awkward and unconvincing account of cyclic history presented in the Coda suggests that the Catholic Church has served its purpose, chaperoning humankind through the worst dangers of the twentieth century. John Faulkner's letter, telling us that the "Revolt of the Castles … began the freedom of the world" (233), suggests that the combination of secular and Protestant dissent has won the day and ushered in a new world of technological advance. But the insistent symbol tells us another story entirely. For the symbol scratched on the castle walls shows that the Fairies are still here. It is their world now; they are the true winners in all of this; the world that has emerged from the Revolt of the Castles is the old way: the way born from the very rocks of the English landscape.

BIBLIOGRAPHY

KEITH ROBERTS

Kiteworld. 1985. London: Gollancz.
Pavane. 1968 [1985]. London: Penguin.
The Chalk Giants. 1974. London: Hutchinson.

SECONDARY SOURCES

Bilson, Fred. 2005. The Colonialist's Fear of Colonisation and the Alternate Worlds of Ward Moore, Philip K. Dick and Keith Roberts. *Foundation* 94 (Summer): 50–63.
Bould, Mark, and Michelle Reid, eds. 2005. *Parietal Games: Critical Writings by and on M. John Harrison*. London: Science Fiction Foundation; Foundation Studies in Science Fiction 5.
Clarke, Jim. 2019. *Science Fiction and Catholicism: The Rise and Fall of the Robot Papacy*. Canterbury: Gylphi.
Hanna, Judith. 1985. Second Glance. *Vector* 126 (June/July): 11.
Hazard, Paul. 1935 [2013]. *The Crisis of the European Mind 1680–1715*. Translated by J. Lewis May. New York: New York Review Books.
Hurst, L.J. 1985. A Timeless Dance: Keith Roberts' *Pavane* Re-examined. *Vector* 124/125 (April–May): 17–19.
Kincaid, Paul. 1982. Of Men and Machines: Keith Roberts interviewed. *Vector* 108 (June): 6–12.
———. 2014. Pavane. In *Call and Response*, 278–299. Harold Wood: Beccon Publications.
Kipling, Rudyard. 1906 [1975]. *Puck of Pook's Hill*. London: Piccolo.
MacCulloch, Diarmaid. 2003. *Reformation: Europe's House Divided, 1490–1700*. London: Allen Lane.
Rowan, Iain. 2001. Pavane. *Infinity Plus*. http://www.infinityplus.co.uk/nonfiction/pavane.htm. Accessed 15 April 2024.
Ruddick, Nicholas. 1989. Flaws in the Timestream: Unity and Disunity in Keith Roberts's Story-Cycles. *Foundation* 45 (Spring): 38–49.
Tawney, R.H. 1926. *Religion and the Rise of Capitalism*. London: Pelican, 1937 edition.

CHAPTER 5

Grief for the Death of Stones

Abstract One review of *Pavane* described it as a love affair with Corfe Castle, and indeed the Castle, as well as the surrounding landscape of the Isle of Purbeck along with Dorset as a whole, plays an essential role in the work. And not just *Pavane*, Roberts's other work would return again and again to the same landscape. The history buried in the ground of Dorset, from the ruins of ancient monuments to the bodies returned to the land, is fundamental to any understanding of the belief structure of *Pavane*. This chapter examines the role of the landscape in the shaping of character, the shaping of beliefs, and hence the shaping of events.

Keywords Purbeck • Dorset • Cerne Giant • Corfe Castle

Lemady, which Keith Roberts insisted is "certainly not an autobiography" (letter to the author, 27 February 1993), is full of stories which we must presume are mostly true in which Roberts and a girlfriend, usually the one identified as Lemady (see Chap. 6), drive down to Dorset, in particular to the Isle of Purbeck and Corfe Castle. In an interview he said: "[T]he first time I went to Corfe Castle I was almost physically shattered, it had such a profound effect ... That place spoke so much of cruelty, oppression, and terror" (Platt: 178). His own stamping ground was Henley, and later

© The Author(s), under exclusive license to Springer Nature
Switzerland AG 2025
P. Kincaid, *Keith Roberts's* Pavane, Palgrave Science Fiction and
Fantasy: A New Canon,
https://doi.org/10.1007/978-3-031-71567-9_5

other towns along the Thames corridor. It was not an area he had any great affection for; throughout *Lemady* he would refuse to name the town. So, he would get away as often as possible, usually to the West Country. He knew Purbeck well, even before he became a writer, and the landscape suffuses his work. Significant parts of *The Furies* are played out there, as are a number of his early stories. But it was *Pavane* in which the landscape came most significantly into play. Graham Hall begins his review: "*Pavane* is not a novel; it's a love-affair with Corfe Castle" (Hall: 23). And the same landscape would play a similar role in *The Chalk Giants*, with the Cerne Giant at nearby Cerne Abbas providing the central image of the novel. Because they occupy the same territory, because the land gives the same emotional and spiritual charge, any discussion of one book will inevitably involve reference to the other.

The landscape of Purbeck, the hills and heaths, the rocks, the ruins, the ancient monuments, takes on a profound and mystical aspect. As Roberts puts it, Corfe Castle seems "to ride not a hill but a flaw in the timestream, a node of quiet from which possibilities might spread out limitless as the journeyings of the sun" (214). This evocation of the pagan past, the sun-worshipping, is deliberate, because the various belief systems explored in Chap. 4 all place their birth within the land itself, while the Catholic Church against which they are conjoined in opposition is invariably presented as alien, the invader, the system that was imposed upon the land but did not emerge from it, and can never be a part of it.

One of the things that unites the central figures in this dance, the ones whose experience illuminates the growing rebellion, is that each one of them is described as if they are themselves part of the landscape. As John Falconer writes right at the end of the novel: "[I]f you are my son, then you are the son of this place too; of its rocks and soil, its sunlight and wind and trees" (236). Unlike the Catholic Church, they cannot be extricated from the hills and rocks and monuments of Dorset. They are themselves, in a way, Dorset stone. Almost literally so, in some cases. Eli Strange, for instance, is described as looking like "the side of a quarried hill" (15), as "clay-coloured" (19), and as "the old granite shell that had called itself Eli Strange" (18). And when he is buried we are told that "[t]he earth took back her own" (11). It is clearly a family trait, because when Eli's son, Jesse, lies upon his own deathbed, he similarly has a "lined, hard face" (125). But it is not just the granite-like stoniness of their faces that we are meant to note, there is also an implied association with the old ways, the ancient beliefs, for Jesse's deathbed is mentioned in the same breath as "the red night plunge of the sun behind the standing stones of the heaths" (129). These are men of Dorset, chiselled from Dorset stone and inescapably tied to the remnants of ancient Dorset beliefs.

Everywhere we turn throughout *Pavane* close attention is paid to the landscape. For instance, Jesse's route on The Lady Margaret takes him from Durnovaria (Dorchester), via the small village of Wool, on to the harbour at Poole, then out of his way to Swanage to meet the barmaid, Margaret. But at the same time that this careful description of the route situates Jesse within a known landscape, so details along the way throw us out of our recognition by pointing out how different this world is. We are in 1968; this was the England that Roberts's first readers lived in and knew intimately, yet Dorchester is a walled town whose gate is guarded by a serjeant with a halberd, while "Poole huddled behind a massive rampart and ditch" (24). This is still a medieval world, and one in which the local authorities have cause to fear attacks that would warrant such historic defences.

Roberts's characters are not figures isolated in a landscape, but rather figures given substance by their landscape. Thus "The Signaller" opens with a long description of the scene—"On either side of the knoll the land stretched in long, speckled sweeps, paling in the frost smoke until the outlines of distant hills blended with the curdled milk of the sky" (51)— before the badly injured body of Rafe is introduced, more as an object in the landscape than as a person, and someone who is fading as the wintery landscape is fading. In a very careful choice of words, Roberts repeatedly refers to the trees around Rafe as a "copse", which of course suggests "corpse"; even the bitter landscape implies death. And Rafe himself, weak and in pain, wants to "just stay quiet and be dead" (52). Rafe's death is thus prefigured in the opening words of the story, and demonstrated by the way he is positioned in the landscape.

In the flashback that provides the bulk of the story we get an image that seems to pave the way for the eventual entry of the Fairy into Rafe's death. As a child, Rafe would climb among the "barrows crowning the windy tops of hills, *hows* where the old dead lay patient with their broken bones" (56) and dream of kings in fur and jewels. In this, we find an echo of another dream in almost exactly the same landscape in *The Chalk Giants*, when Marck dreams that "I *was* the grain, and earth, and creeping things upon it. And mist and sky, the stones the Giants placed between the hills. I was the land, Miri, and the land was me" (Roberts 1974: 245). In old religions the king would often undergo a symbolic marriage to the land, but Roberts has carried that notion forwards in time and democratised it, so in the modern day of *Pavane* everyone who would go against the dictates of the Church, who would advocate a new, individual, protestant way must similarly marry themselves to the ancient hills and hill forts of England. "The land is where the past resides, and in the past is strength and purity while in the future is only mystery and terror" (Kincaid 2005: 61). This lies behind the tragedy that is the ending of *The Chalk Giants* when, after a sequence of stories of death and rebirth, the final story ends with the arrival of a new ruler to unite the land under a new religion that is cognate with Christianity. It looks like a happy ending, but is not, "for the religion stems from a martyred man, not from the land, and the new king is not married to the land; the hills and the sea will be empty". Ahead lie the same patterns we have seen before, in *Pavane* as much as in *The Chalk Giants*. "Time and again, Roberts tells us that history is cyclic, that we are doomed to repeat the same mistakes, commit the same horrors" (Kincaid 2005: 61). As we see in Rafe's vision, both Roberts's version of Balder and the Christos experience the same death, hanging upon a tree, but Balder's death nourishes the land, the death of Christos brings only war and bloodshed.

Connection to the land, therefore, an emotional engagement with the past that is buried in the very stones that form the hills, is essential for those who would draw the strength necessary for dissent. In a later story, "The Big Fans" (1977), the narrator leaves England at the end, and in commenting on the story I noted: "For Roberts, as deeply and intrinsically attached to the landscape as he is, the notion of leaving England has a cataclysmic finality to it" (Kincaid 2001: 21). In *Pavane*, only two of the characters actually leave the country. Becky begins to lose a sense of who she is and where she belongs, and returns to conflict. Brother John sails away to his death.

If "Brother John" is the emotional and spiritual heart of *Pavane*, it is hardly surprising that, as a lithographer, the very tools of his trade are stones. The first thing we see in the story is "walls of rough-dressed ashlar, stone slabs stood in line" (87). And our first sight of Brother John himself is of him using boxes of silver sand to grind "a slab of limestone some two feet long by four or more inches thick" (87). For John, "[T]he colour and texture of the stones and the many ways of working them appealed to the latent craftsman in him" (92). They also tie him to the land and to the past. Given that John only joined the church because it was the one way he could pursue his love of art, then his faith is expressed in the way he works the stone. But when he witnesses the Inquisition at work with "the cut legs and arms, the severed heads, the bodies broken on the wheel, pierced and burned by the hot iron chairs" (100), he sees them working upon human beings the same way he works on stone, and that represents a very different faith, one he cannot share. In the end it is, of course, significant that it is witnessing a blind quarryman working himself to death by cutting stones out of the ground, that prompts his final vision. And the wife of the quarryman, who is beside John to witness her husband's sacrifice, was "stone herself among the grey stone hills" (113). John decides then to set out for Rome, which he identifies as "the Rock ... the Throne of Peter" (116), a name that is, as we know, derived from *Petros* meaning stone. John's entire journey, therefore, has taken him from stone to stone to stone. And the last thing we see, after his boat has overturned, is waves that "slapped at the upturned keel of a boat, urging it back gently towards the land" (117).

The village where John experiences his final vision is described thus: "The cottages were of grey stone storm-shuttered and desolate. The few trees that grew were stunted and low, carved by the wind into strange smooth shapes; their branches leaning towards the roofs as if for protection" (108). As if the village has grown out of the land, and the land has gown together with the village. But we meet this village again later, or at least its near neighbour, because here "Heresy walked like a spectre, blew in on the sea wind; till a man saw the old monk himself, grim-faced and empty-eyed, stalking the cliff-tops in his tattered gown" (171). "The White Boat" occurs long enough after "Brother John" for John himself to have become a ghost, a folk memory emerging out of the cliff top, and the village has gone from grey to black.

Nothing in *Pavane* equates character and landscape as vividly and as insistently as "The White Boat", because here the black rock, the black soil, the black air seeps into every part of everyone who lives there. The bay was black because the sea ate at the coal-bearing rock and spread a fine dark grit over everything. "The grass had taken the colour of it and the little houses that stood mean-shouldered glaring at the water; the boats and jetties had taken it, and the brambles and gorse; even the rabbits that thumped across the cliff paths on summer evenings seemed to have something of the same dusky hue" (153). And Becky becomes aware that "the people too had taken the colour of the place; an airborne, invisible smut had changed them all" (158). In other words, everything, living and inanimate, had taken on the blackness; it is a "wild, mournful place ... a shadow of old sin" (154). Becky's loneliness is described as "an oppression born of the gentle miles of summer water, the tall blackness of the headlands, the stone fingers of the ledges pushing out to sea" (155); it is born of the landscape. And when Becky's father beats her after she returns from the boat, "Her body had sprung from rock and shale, the gloomy vastness of the fields; the strap fell not on her but on the headlands, the rocks, the sea" (169).

The White Boat, because of its colour and its free movement, is a glaring contrast to everything in her life. The other villagers treat it with suspicion, presumably they are aware that it is smuggling and therefore dangerous; but Becky associates it with becoming adult, the "slicing shock and redness [that] turned her instantly into a woman" (157). The first period, coming with the shock of cold water as she swims out to the White Boat, is echoed in *The Chalk Giants* when Mata experiences her first period as she dives into water, when "it seemed in her delirium a great truth came to her … and life ended, in a wonderful soaring flight" (Roberts 1974: 97). But if her quixotic swim to the boat brings Becky to womanhood, it also seems "to cut her off from earthly contact" (160). She means nothing to the smugglers on board the boat, for meaning she needs connection to the land.

The importance of this connection, the way it links to the history within the land, is illustrated by one brief incident. Becky collects ammonites, but is scolded by Father Anthony because "if God created the rocks in seven days then He created those markings too" (155). The Church once again demonstrating its alien nature, its disconnection from the land and its history. In both the other stories within the cycle that focus on female characters there is a similar, visceral connection to the long history tied up in the rocks. Margaret is taken up into the hills by Jesse, who digs out a fossil from the rocks and when she held it to her ear she heard "the noise the years made, all the millions of them shut inside buzzing to get free" (128/9). And when she decides to turn away from the Church, Margaret has a vision in which she sees "Corfe loom at her with its skull face … the cliffs tall in the droning wind" (146). While Eleanor once "took a flake of shale and pressed it to her throat and cried, and said that day she was made right through of stone, dark and stern as the Kimmeridge cliffs and as indomitable" (189).

Time itself is condensed into the landscape: to be at one with the land and with all its features, the fossils, the ruins, the ancient monuments, is to be at one with all that has gone to make England. So, for the characters, "their awareness of the land, in the most significant cases their marriage to the land, shapes their beliefs, their morality, even the stories they enact" (Kincaid 2005: 59). It is a deeply conservative (though only intermittently Conservative) view of the world, or more precisely of England. And it is almost invariably England of which Roberts writes. By my estimate, "no more than nine short stories out of his 120-plus stories and ten novels" (Kincaid 2005: 59) are set outside England. People are indistinguishable from the place that made them. Becky dreams (yet another dream in a book full of dreams) of all the people she knows melting "chaotically into the landscape till the cliffs were bodies and bones and old beseeching hands, teeth, and eyes and crumbling ancient foreheads" (158). Here death does not translate one into heaven, but into the stones from which the Fairies and the ancient gods emerge. In the magazine version of "Corfe Gate" the visitor, Paul, happens upon Eleanor's gravestone, and as he clears the grass from around the stone, "as I touched the grass some bird burst from it and rushed into the sky" (Roberts 1966: 68), new life springing from a stone, spirit rising into the air. And when Margaret has her vision of the Old One, he tells her: "Look into solid earth, into rock, and see the galaxies of all Creation" (147), all the skies above are there under our feet.

As people go back to the earth and the Old Ones emerge from the earth, so all of time, past and future, is contained within the land. As Margaret wonders to herself, could "the Things that knocked and fretted, the haunters, *the Old Ones* ... Snatch her out of Space and Time" (131). The answer, of course, is no because both space and time are inherent in the Old Ones. But rather than being outside of space and time, the landscape places you firmly within it, and it is from this that visions emerge. And this whole story cycle is visionary, told through memories and daydreams. Rafe's story is made almost entirely of memories and visions; John's story builds inexorably to his great vision; as Margaret sits by Jesse's deathbed, her vision changes: "From the past she had moved to the future, or to some Time that had never been and never would be" (146); for Becky, the return of the White Boat is as if it had been "nothing but a vision or a dream, lacking weight and substance" (156); and the seneschal, John Faulkner, tells Eleanor stories of "the times before there were castles on our hilltops and before the world knew anything of churches" (202/3). So much of *Pavane* is about dreams and visions, but there is nothing airy or ethereal about them. These are dreams of blood and stone, the solidity of history and the land from which that history emerges. The more the characters and their stories are tied to the earth, the more visionary the book becomes.

The landscape of Dorset across whose hills and heaths and valleys this story is played out is a realm filled with monuments of the past, from the stone circle of Avebury to the chalk giant above Cerne Abbas. The longer these monuments have survived, the more power and mystery they have accumulated. But this doesn't just feed into the atmosphere of the story cycle; it shapes the way events occur and are regarded within the story. The dissent fomented by Brother John is marked by his followers burning the Pope "in effigy at Woodhenge and Badbury Rings" (102), and later John's staff is said to have flowered "like the staff of the blessed Joseph at Glastonbury" (108), while soldiers search for him "from Sarum Rings to the Valley of the Giant at Cerne" (108). At every stage, the rebellion is inextricably associated with ancient monuments.

Meanwhile, the Cardinal Archbishop of Londinium represents the Church as "stretched like a glittering blanket, a counterpane of cloth of gold, across the body of a giant" (104). English mythology has long represented the landscape in terms of giants, from Gog and Magog, the guardian giants of London, to the giants' dance that would become Stonehenge. Another stone circle, at Avebury, is linked to the giants' dance of Stonehenge when Rafe recalls the "gambolling diamond-shapes … where the stones danced against the morning sun" (56). These monuments, and their associational connection to the idea of a monumental past, are vitally important to Roberts. When Lemady writes that all the stones of Stonehenge came from Prescelly he has to correct her: only the Bluestones were hauled from Prescelly: "The great inner ring, the towering trilithons, were quarried from the sarsen sheet that once overlaid all Wiltshire" (Roberts 1997: 9). But even in this correctness, the precision is tinged with the romance, the magic, of the past; he reacts with fury to prosaic suggestions that Stonehenge is a computer, that it can be decoded. So the Archbishop's image is prescient: the Cerne Abbas giant is made actual as the representation of the land, England being envisaged as a sleeping giant being awakened to bring freedom "in concert with the Fairies, the tutelary spirits of the land" (Ruddick 1989: 15). Everything that happens within the novel is thus inextricably tied to the land and to the Fairies who are the spirits of the land. It is a persistent element in Roberts's work. In the late, semi-autobiographical novel, *Gráinne*, the avatar for Roberts, Alistair Bevan (a pseudonym he had used frequently), visits a ruined castle and "knew himself to be at rest; future and past in gentle, perfect balance ... and yet his eyes were open. They marked the moving grass, dark waves that ran across; in time its rustling returned. Yet now there seemed something more; a Presence, in the brilliant afternoon. As if the stones themselves were focus for some force" (Roberts 1987: 161). We could almost be observing Rafe slowly becoming aware of the presence of the fairy.

The fact that Roberts himself, or at least a lightly fictionalised version of Roberts, responds to the landscape in exactly the same way as the characters in *Pavane* is significant: this is a very personal book, a book in which the author's own investment in the monuments and landscapes of Dorset is played out in the drama of his story. David Matless, in his study of *Landscape and Englishness* (2016), considers among other things "themes of dissidence and foreignness which feature in ... [a] ... search for English origins" (Matless: 164). In such a search "Avebury remained as a symbol of ancient English peace" (Matless: 166), and "If society emerged from the soil, then authority was to be similarly grounded" (Matless: 167). *Pavane* seems to put each of these notions into practice. There is a nativist society emergent, literally, from the stones in the ground that expresses a growing dissent from a foreign authority, the Catholic Church, meanwhile holding up Avebury and other ancient monuments, from the Cerne Abbas giant to the ruins of Corfe Castle, as symbols of all that true Englishness aspires towards.

Also drawing on Matless, Roger Luckhurst associates Roberts with a sense of "melancholia articulated through English landscapes" (Luckhurst: 176), noting how a sense of melancholic loss is mapped onto the most symbolic landscapes in England. This personification of landscape charged with mystical and historic resonance is a commonplace in much English science fiction. Luckhurst points in particular to the Wessex of Christopher Priest's *A Dream of Wessex* (1977), and the ancient Herefordshire woodlands of Robert Holdstock's *Mythago Wood* (1984). We might also think of the new religion arising out of the fractured landscape in Richard Cowper's White Bird of Kinship sequence. But the obvious standard bearer of this form of melancholia is Keith Roberts, who time and again turned to iconic West Country landscapes, Salisbury Plain in *The Furies*, Purbeck and the Cerne Abbas Giant in *The Chalk Giants*, but most of all the central role played by Corfe Castle in *Pavane*.

Roberts clearly loved the landscape of Dorset, particularly around Purbeck, Cerne Abbas, and most notably Corfe. He wrote about it with "an eloquence, a poetry, which suggests a deep and passionate commitment to the land. Yet he is forever tearing it apart" (Kincaid 2001: 23). In *The Furies* it has been torn apart by atomic weapons; in *The Chalk Giants*, another novel of nuclear dread, there is a sea where the maps suggest land should be; in *Molly Zero* the country is cut up by barbed wire and command posts. In his entry on Roberts in the first edition of the *Encyclopedia of Science Fiction* (1979), John Clute points out that "a clear hatred of violence and savagery sometimes emerges uncomfortably in images of pain and mutilation" (Clute 1979: 500). Roberts has admitted that there is a lot of truth in the remark, though the comment has been omitted from subsequent editions of the Encyclopedia. But the mutilation is applied to the landscape even more than it is to the characters. It is part of the melancholy of the books: he is drawn to the ruin of Corfe Castle as much as he is repelled by the war that created the ruin. Like Brother John, he cannot look away from the torture. Time and again the shattered land represents the moral dilemma faced by the characters, and the loss of control they face.

All the way through *Pavane* we see damaged people. Jesse kills the man who had been his best friend along with the rest of the *routiers* by blowing up the last waggon in his train: "scythe[ing] the valley clear of life" (47–8). In order to become a signaller, Rafe has to spend a physically arduous day transmitting the Book of Nehemiah, a day in which "the pain began. In the shoulders, in the back, in the buttocks and calves. His world narrowed; he saw neither the sun nor the distant sea. … With fatigue came a trance-like state in which logic was suspended, the reasons for actions lost" (69). Brother John, of course, has to witness the cruelty of the Inquisition, after which "his face had lost its colouring, acquiring instead a greyish sheen like the face of a corpse" (97), he has lost weight, his clothes are frayed, he stares blankly ahead, vacant-faced. Like John, Margaret also witnesses torment; this time when old William "lost half his fingers in a workshop lathe" (131) and she had run to see and to help: "She hated, she sickened, but she just had to *see*" (132). And the very first time we see Eleanor she fires a huge cannon point blank at Sir Henry and his men. Pain, injury, torment, blood are ever-present, and it is difficult to tell if this is the blood of Balder that nourishes the land, or the blood of Christos that brings more war. Yet for once in Roberts the violence and mutilation seem to be confined to the human characters, while the land itself remains whole. But none of this violence is entirely separate from the land. It is done to further the aims of those who emerge from the land, it is done to honour the land, and it is done for the land's cause. Here the people take the place of the landscape in suffering and in witnessing suffering, but these people are part of the land; they come from the land and act on its behalf. They take on themselves the suffering of the land, but it is the torment they must go through to achieve the release, the modernity, they aspire towards. As John Faulkner concludes his letter to his son: "[D]o not grieve, for the deaths of stones" (236).

BIBLIOGRAPHY

KEITH ROBERTS

"Corfe Gate" (Original Version). 1966. *Impulse* Vol. 1, Issue 5: 7–68.
Gráinne. 1987. Salisbury: Kerosina Publications.
Lemady: Episodes of a Writer's Life. 1997. Gillette, NJ: Wildside Press.
Molly Zero. 1980. London: Gollancz.
Pavane. 1968 [1985]. London: Penguin.
The Chalk Giants. 1974. London: Hutchinson.
The Furies. 1966. London: Rupert Hart-Davis.

SECONDARY SOURCES

Clute, John. 1979. Keith Roberts. In *The Encyclopedia of Science Fiction*, 1st ed., 499–500. London: Granada.
Hall, Graham. 1969. Pavane. *Speculation* 22 (April): 23–24.
Kincaid, Paul. 2001. Future Historical: The Fiction of Keith Roberts. *Steam Engine Time* 3 (December): 20–24.
———. 2005. Landscape in the Fiction of Keith Roberts. *Foundation* 93 (Spring): 59–66.
Luckhurst, Roger. 2005. *Science Fiction.* Cambridge: Polity Press.
Matless, David. 2016 [2019]. *Landscape and Englishness*, Second Expanded Edition. London: Reaktion Books.
Platt, Charles. 1982. *Dream Makers: Volume II.* Strange Particle Press. Revised edition: 2021.
Ruddick, Nicholas. 1989. Flaws in the Timestream: Unity and Disunity in Keith Roberts's Story-Cycles: Part Two. *Foundation* 46 (Autumn): 14–26.

CHAPTER 6

Equivalents of a Dream

Abstract This concluding chapter looks at two figures who are inextricably important in the character of *Pavane*, and who would go on to play a similarly vital role in much of the fiction that came after. These two are the artist, Paul Nash, probably the most important artistic influence in Roberts's life and the person who perhaps introduced Roberts to the symbolic importance of Dorset; and the figure dubbed the multigirl, who would represent the eternal and universal feminine in all of Roberts's work.

Keywords Paul Nash · Dorset · Multigirl · Primitive Heroine

Two figures need to be examined in relation to *Pavane* though the role they play would not be restricted to this one book. Neither is here addressed directly, but by considering the parts they play it is possible to tease out some of the threads that not only bind the various parts of *Pavane* together but that tie it to the author's other books. One of these figures is unnamed and plays no part in the measures of the dance but was an important inspiration behind the whole thing. The other has too many names, though we have no way of knowing her real or original name, and was a very different inspiration for the work.

The first of these was the artist, Paul Nash (1889–1946). Nash, an official war artist in both World Wars, and in between notable for producing a series of symbolic and often surreal landscapes, was probably the most important artist in Roberts's personal iconography. He has said that "I knew the work of Paul Nash, the English landscape painter, long before I took up the formal study of art" (Roberts 1997: 50), and in response to an unsympathetic review of *The Chalk Giants* by David I. Masson, emphasised that "such symbolism as exists in the book is drawn not from my own 'turgid' imagination but from the work of the quasi-mystical painter Paul Nash" (Roberts 1975: 68). I will be attempting to show how much Nash influenced the visual imagery that runs through this work and later ones, but it is worth pointing out how much Nash's vision of Dorset coincides with Roberts's own. Indeed, although he nowhere says as much, one might wonder whether Roberts was first drawn to Dorset because of Nash.

In 1936, Nash produced the *Shell Guide to* Dorset, and in it "presented a landscape that was fundamentally at odds with conventional perceptions of quaint England … [and which] … subtly questioned the progress of Western civilisation and its assumed superiority over things perceived as primitive" (Fill: 49). It is an approach to the county that could almost stand as a description of *Pavane*. In his guidebook, Nash describes the county as "scarred and furrowed" by events of the past (quoted, Fill: 49), and again that sense of history emerging out of the human imprint on the landscape is what shapes the narrative in *Pavane*. We don't know whether Roberts had read Nash's guidebook to Dorset, though given his attraction to both the artist and the county I would be surprised if he had not. And it feels as though Nash had prepared Roberts to look for precisely the sort of story that the Corfe barmaid presented to him.

The fascination with the past that runs through Nash's work includes a consistent interest in fossils, and in the bones of ancient Britons unearthed by Mortimer Wheeler during his excavations at Maiden Castle; people literally raised out of the ground. And we have seen consistent references to fossils throughout *Pavane*, as when Becky collects ammonites, or when Margaret listens to the sounds the years make. What's more, Nash's painting, which Roger Cardinal describes as "[a] metaphoric way of constructing landscapes and objects, one so intense as to stimulate the process of metamorphosis" (Cardinal: 48), often incorporated aspects of ancient monuments, such as the Badbury Rings, the Avebury stone circle, and Corfe Castle, which he drew multiple times. Although not themselves images of devastation, these scenes often evoke a sense of disquiet much like his paintings of churned landscapes and shattered trees from his time in the trenches. They are places weighed down with a sense of history, long, hard, and often cruel. The landscape that Roberts presents in *Pavane*, which so often references the same ancient monuments, evokes much the same disquiet, though here the harshness of the past has been reborn in the story's present. In a letter to me, he said of Nash: "*Pavane* is soaked with his imagery ... [though] ... it's not specifically acknowledged" (quoted, Kincaid 2014: 299).

Sometimes this imagery just takes the form of setting the story in the landscape that Nash painted. Sometimes there is something more elusive about the influence. Although an artist himself—Roberts produced a string of visually arresting covers for both *Science Fantasy/Impulse* and *New Worlds*—he insisted: "I've never been an artist in the 'fine arts' sense; I'm a commercial visualiser, finisher and copywriter" and therefore claimed there was no connection between his art and his writing, he was not trying to replicate in words the paintings of Paul Nash. Yet he went on to say that "What I did think had a profound effect [on my writing] was the art *training* ... [because] ... Visual perception alters certainty" (Kincaid 1982, 6). It is, therefore, the visual perception, what he sees and how he sees it, that comes to him via Paul Nash. Thus, when we first encounter Rafe amid a stark clump of trees, the scene it calls to mind is the Oxfordshire landscape of the Wittenham Clumps, which Nash painted repeatedly. Nash recorded the horrors of the First World War with the same obsessive attention to detail that Brother John devotes to the horrors of the Inquisition. And when, as a child, Eleanor watches the waves "marching in their violet ranks to break against the ancient cliffs" (188) the image was inspired by Nash's "Landscape from a Dream".

The same influences, even more explicit, are present in Roberts's other great mosaic novel set in the same ancient, mystical landscape, *The Chalk Giants*. There, early in the novel in a story whose title, "The Sun Over a Low Hill", could be affixed to a variety of Nash's paintings from the 1930s, we are told: "He discovered the Hardy novels, and in time the painter Nash; the hills and trees and standing stones, flowers that broke from their moorings to sail the sky, fossils that reared in ghostly anger from the rocks. Suns rolling their millstones of golden grain; and it seemed he heard, far off and far too late, the shock of distant armies" (Roberts 1974: 21). That belated shock of distant armies is an echo we have heard already in the paintings of Paul Nash, the memories of the trenches suffusing even his peacetime work; but it is something also that arises out of the ancient landscape in both *Pavane* and *The Chalk Giants*. And these are discoveries that could be identified with Roberts himself as much as with the luckless protagonist of *The Chalk Giants*, Stan Potts. This is a passage that could be at home just as readily in *Pavane*, the way the art is redolent of the land is an important point in understanding the artistic vision behind the novel. And it is important to note that key characters come to embody "a quality suffusing the whole landscape, a numinosity" (Ruddick 1989b: 19). It is worth noting also that the influence of Nash is specifically linked to the importance of cyclic history in the structure of the book. Thus, of *The Chalk Giants*, Roberts says that "Nash's sun wheel … is turning again; there is to be more burning and slaughter, in the name of yet another God of Love" (Roberts 1975: 71).

"Nash, as a landscape painter, strove to provide a link between landscape and mythology; the old myths of Britain arose from the countryside and are inseparable from it, touching it with magic as they touch it with the physical signs of standing stones, stone circles, chalk figures, all the scenic devices that recur like a Greek chorus throughout Roberts's work" (Kincaid 2014: 295). Nash, of course, is not the only British painter to plough this particular quasi-mystical furrow. Andrew M. Butler, for instance, points out that alongside Nash, "Roberts' work continues a neo-romantic tradition which can be traced back to Samuel Palmer, Thomas Bewick and [William] Blake" (Butler: 109). Whatever the influence, what is undeniable is that it has given a painterly quality to the prose that numerous critics have picked up on. Charles Platt notes that "the scenery is more than graphic—you can smell the damp earth and feel the texture of every rock" (Platt: 174). For Graham Hall, this imagistic richness comes across as overwriting: "His prose is a stew, as thick and luscious as a Brahms symphony. … But he writes with the conviction of a lover" (Hall: 24). While in his review of *Pavane*, Christopher Priest considered that the writing has "a richness of tone and detail that has a visual imagistic power of panavision proportions" (Priest 1968: 15).

After *The Chalk Giants*, Roberts did not set his work so explicitly in Dorset, except on very rare occasions. There is a curious 1972 story, "I Lose Medea", originally published as by Alistair Bevan, in which we witness a ghostly siege of a medieval castle by a force that seems to date from the First World War, equipped with eighteen-pounder guns and "a steam traction engine with half-tracks" (Roberts 1976: 199), which feels almost as if we are looking back at *Pavane* from outside the story cycle, with a reference to Nash's First World War experiences thrown in for good measure. But the sense, derived from Nash, that people are best seen as part of the landscape, indeed that they and their history emerge from the land, continues. In one of his poems from the 1980s, for instance, "A Downland Haunting", set partly in Berkshire, partly in the Chilterns, Roberts says:

> You follow the eye's shapes; somewhere a hint, a dream,
> Limned by gold wheat, a hip, a thigh, organic.
> A slim girl might be lying on her side,
> Lost in the contours. (Roberts 1987b: 41)

The "gold wheat" perhaps another reference to Nash's "Solstice of the Sunflower", with its golden sun-like wheel rolling across the landscape. And Roberts's late, semi-autobiographical novel, *Gráinne*, draws much of its power from revisiting familiar ancient landscapes, from Dorset to Oxfordshire, to Ireland. Even where not acknowledged, as it mostly isn't, the influence of Paul Nash is inescapable, not just in the painterly way the land is described, but in the role it plays in delineating the characters.

Which brings us to the second key figure that needs to be discussed, the so-called multigirl. But here, too, the influence of Nash is felt. In one of the stories in *The Chalk Giants*, Mata, an iteration of the multigirl, causes a chalk giant to be engraved upon a hillside. In one moment, therefore, she embodies the vital importance of the land, the role of the multigirl as genius loci, and the power of art. All of these things come together in Roberts, so it is impossible to talk about the eternal feminine, the land, or art without referring each to the other.

To examine the role of the multigirl throughout the fiction of Keith Roberts is to step into an arena that is a minefield of contradictions and complexities. Roberts was unusual as a male science fiction writer of his era in that he would frequently make women not only his protagonists but also the most active and powerful characters in the work. As Charles Platt says: "Many of his stories have featured young, forceful females" (Platt, 180). But in response Roberts pointed out, this isn't quite accurate, he writes as much about men as he does women; it's just that there was a chauvinist side to science fiction, particularly at the time he was writing, and so the sheer number of women in his work, treated as human beings rather than angels or demons, made them stand out. This is something that we see not only in the three last measures of *Pavane* and in *The Chalk Giants*, but also in *The Inner Wheel* (1970), *Molly Zero* (1980), the various

Kaeti stories, and *Gráinne*. He once told me that the reason so many male writers failed in their portrayal of women is that when they wrote of a woman walking across a room they would dwell on the feel of the skirt swinging against her leg, the sound of her nylon-clad thighs rubbing against each other. Whereas Roberts would simply say she walked across the room. Yet if that seems to rescue the woman from the male gaze, his own descriptions of women would often centre upon her sexual character-istics. Moreover, few if any of his female characters were individualised, he presented them rather as aspects of some universal, archetypal form. All women, effectively, are the same woman, and she belongs to one of two archetypes: the multigirl or the Primitive Heroine. So at one and the same moment he might give her strength and take away her individuality.

The Primitive Heroine, or P.H., a term he took from Robert Holdstock, has "presence. When she walks into a room, heads turn. More than that; you can feel her vibes on the back of your neck, like the radiation from an electric fire. You might not know her name, you might not have seen her enter; but you know she's *there*" (Roberts 1988: 7). She is, therefore, defined by the male gaze; the "you" in this passage is always the one doing the looking, not the one being looked upon. The Primitive Heroine, as typified by the teenage witch, Anita, or by Pete in *The Furies*, tends to be young, quick-witted, tomboyish, appears untamed in manner or dress, and is, of course, sexy, "the archetypal dollybird character" (Roberts 1997. 148) I think the use of 1960s language even in a passage written in the 1990s speaks volumes about Roberts's perception of this archetype. When he defines the character of the Primitive Heroine it is primarily in terms of appearance: "[S]he isn't conventionally beautiful, sometimes not even particularly pretty. ... She tends to be trim rather than spectacular; long in the leg, neat as regards bottom and bust" (Roberts 1988: 6). Naturally, she is not academically inclined, but she is street smart, active, and "[h]er mental makeup is curious; unpredictable, wayward perhaps, but never *dull*" (Roberts 1988: 8), while her "attitude to sex is as forthright and refreshing as the rest of her views" (Roberts 1988: 11). That reference to "dollybird" was no accident because, in many ways, from her patched jeans to her no-nonsense sexuality, the Primitive Heroine is a revenant from the free-love 1960s who has not changed in the subsequent decades. Indeed, the fashions of later decades, from piercings to the shaved heads of punk, are regarded (by Roberts, though he imposes this view on the P.H.) with disgust. And the P.H. is herself a multigirl who recurs through-out history; Roberts sees her recreated in medieval carvings, in the paintings of Bosch and Botticelli and Modigliani, in the illustrations of Aubrey Beardsley and Alphonse Mucha, in the music of the *Carmina Burana* and Janacek. The key to this fairly blatant object of desire is that she is always the same no matter where or when you might encounter her.

In contrast, the multigirl is different wherever she appears, always taking on the appropriate appearance and characteristics for the context in which she finds herself. Her definitive appearance is as the barmaid, Martine, who recurs in different guises throughout *The Chalk Giants*. Roberts attributes the term "multigirl" to Michael Coney. In my 1982 interview he said of Becky in "The White Boat" that she is "actually the first appearance of the character Michael Coney later christened 'multigirl', a phrase I still rather like" (Kincaid 1982: 10). I have since been unable to find anywhere that Coney said this in print, though he may not necessarily have been talking about *The Chalk Giants*, as Roberts went on to talk of her as "a sort of all-purpose standby character on whom I felt I could rely; a little like Mike Moorcock's great Cathy Cornelius perhaps, a fictional lady I've always loved dearly" (Kincaid 1982: 10).

Roberts's insistence that Becky was the first appearance of the multigirl is, to say the least, disingenuous. Certainly Becky was a multigirl, an identification signalled by the fact that she experiences her first period, which stands in the story for a sort of sexual awakening, as she swims towards the White Boat, just as Mata, in "The God House", the fourth episode in *The Chalk Giants*, experiences her first period in water. There is, therefore, a link between Becky and at least one of the incarnations of Martine in *The Chalk Giants*. But she is neither the only nor even the first of such replications. Becky and Martine were both based on the same person, "a barmaid at a Dorset pub I frequented" (Roberts 1986, 7). But that Dorset barmaid had already inspired the character of the barmaid Margaret in "The Lady Margaret", and her daughter, Margaret Strange, and Eleanor, and finally, reverting to her original role, as the barmaid who encounters our protagonist in the Coda, the girl who found a secret way into the castle and who would "sit up there and imagine it was all mine" (235) just as the original real-life barmaid had imagined herself as Lady Mary Bankes, the defender of Corfe Castle. There is, it would seem, only one multigirl, and she ranges freely across both *Pavane* and *The Chalk Giants* and even in "Our Lady of Desperation" (1979), where she plays "the dangerously attractive nymphet who was really the catalyst for the entire piece" (Kincaid 1982: 10).

Of course an "attractive nymphet" might also apply to young Becky, and both she and the character in "Our Lady of Desperation" might thus be described as Primitive Heroines. But really there is nothing to distinguish the two archetypes; there is a sense that for Roberts there was only one archetype to which all women conformed, an eternal feminine who might change on a whim from Primitive Heroine to multigirl.

Lemady, the recurring if otherwise anonymous female figure in his idiosyncratic memoir, is a distinct model for both the P.H. and the multigirl. When she first appears, draped beside Roberts in his sporty Triumph Spitfire, she is "wearing light blue slacks, a vivid matching blouse. Her blonde hair flows forward in a heavy cloud. Sunglasses are propped on her nose" (Roberts 1997: 5). But there is a multifaceted aspect to her character: "Her independence of spirit gives way at times to a seeming desire for compliance, a need to play second string; though it is as dangerous as it would be undesirable to take her attitude for granted. She is made up of opposites; withdrawn by nature, she can still play the Scarlet Woman" (Roberts 1997: 6). But even this is liable to change, at one point her hair is "brown, red-gold, near white" (Roberts 1997: 9), at another she is "five eleven" (Roberts 1997: 30), yet later he reports: "She's five ten now, and Swedish ... the schoolboy's dream of home" (Roberts 1997: 80). One gets the impression that she is not one person, but that every woman he encounters is somehow cast in the role of Lemady—"Lemady seems endlessly to recreate herself" (Roberts 1997: 51)—or rather she is the source of every woman he writes, "a memory bank is building from which I am to draw, time and again" (Roberts 1997: 9). He specifically equates Lemady with *Molly Zero* and with Libby Maynard from *The Inner Wheel* though he insists that Gráinne only partly draws on Lemady. And this everywoman even reaches back in time, taking on a multifaceted role throughout history, in fact a role embedded in the folklore of the land. "She told me once she couldn't remember how many times she had been Lucia Queen; the ancient, magic creature who walks on the shortest day, to call back the light" (Roberts 1997: 81). As John Clute puts it, writing of a later incarnation of this figure in *Gráinne*, Roberts composed "an anguished submission to Woman as intoxicant and succubus, and as saviour of these Isles one day" (Clute 1995: 21). This is so close in spirit to the barmaid who told Roberts that she was the reincarnation of Lady Mary Bankes, and who thus inspired *Pavane*, that it seems to be a defining characteristic of womanhood from Roberts's perspective. All women must embody all other women, past and present, so that any female character in his work must take on the aspect of all other women, as he says of Kaeti: "Every pretty, spirited young girl I ever met forms part of her in a way"

(Roberts 1997: 99). Asked if Kaeti was a version of the multigirl, Roberts replied: "Sort of. ... I think they're fantasies that could each have a psychological explanation—so what is new?" (Kincaid 1986, 3).

Whether these various female characters, all necessarily young, pretty, and spirited, are evocations of Roberts's own fantasies is probably beside the point, but they are all Primitive Heroines who are also and inevitably multigirls. They are everywoman, the eternal feminine, because the goddess is our closest association with the land, with the past, with everything that makes us. In an autobiography crowded with female acquaintances there would appear to be none to whom the terms young, sexy, spirited do not apply. They are, so far as Roberts is concerned, "the very nature of woman herself ... [and] ... the same in any age" (Roberts 1997: 147). Which is why they must play the most active and spirited role in *Pavane*, in *The Chalk Giants*, in *Molly Zero*, in *Gráinne*, and elsewhere, because they are in themselves the representatives of past and present, because they are in themselves the embodiment of everything that we might desire.

Following a criticism that Lady Eleanor wears patterned nylons, Roberts provides a telling detail that illustrates both the spirit of *Pavane* and the role of women in his personal mythology. The reason that Lady Eleanor wore patterned nylons was because "the lass who sparked off the whole idea wore patterned nylons. ... Grab that, and you've grabbed the very heart of the book, because everything sprang from that. North and south, forward and back, up and down. ... A girl *can* wear nylons, and defend a castle; because girls, and women, never change" (Roberts 1986, 7). This is oddly empowering and disempowering at the same time. It insists that women can achieve anything, but at the cost of not being an individual, at the cost of being a Primitive Heroine or multigirl who is identical with every other Primitive Heroine or multigirl from the beginning of time to its end.

In the quasi-autobiographical *Gráinne*, Roberts identifies the central male character with himself by the simple expedient of calling him by one of Roberts's own pseudonyms, Alistair Bevan. But it is the female character, Gráinne, who is confident and in control, while Bevan makes few choices, and indeed actively avoids them. Women have the power, but only by embodying all women.

Nicholas Ruddick speculates that the reason Roberts created this multiform embodiment of everywoman was his realisation "that a partially deindividualized female character—the 'multigirl'—was better able to bear the symbolic freight of his new concern than more deliberately individualized male characters" (Ruddick 1989a, 44). This doesn't quite explain why women must conform to this continuity of their role while male characters are necessarily individualised. As I've said here, part of what makes the multigirl is Roberts incorporating aspects of the different women he knew as if he can only see them as part of some all-encompassing whole. But Ruddick goes on to consider that women disempowered by the patriarchy are thus "more likely to offer a truly countervailing principle" and one that is "more symbolically connected to the earth, and hence to its literal manifestation in the land" (Ruddick 1989a, 45), and this does tie in (see above) with Roberts equating the multigirl with the folklore of the land and the saviour of the isles. It is notable that the first three *Pavane* measures focus on male characters who have visions of the way to go without successfully putting them into practice. But as the story moves towards overt rebellion, the focus shifts towards female characters—Margaret, Becky, and Eleanor—as if they better embody the land rising up in rebellion. Thus, with Becky, the white boat is seen, by its contrast to the black land, as the embodiment of freedom. But once Becky reaches the boat she is out of place, a woman alone in a tightly male world, and, perhaps more significantly, being at sea she is disconnected from the land. The boat is modernity, the land is antiquity, and it is from the deep past, echoes of the previous cycles of the world, and the symbolic landscapes of Woodhenge and Corfe and such, that these women are imbued with the will to rebellion. The boat has to be warned off at the end; it has to escape the trap, because the promise of freedom must be maintained, but that alone is not the source of the rebellion. The illicit technology that the boat is smuggling in will aid the rebellion, but it will not be the cause of rebellion.

Repeatedly throughout this book I have discussed *Pavane* and *The Chalk Giants* as if they resonate off each other. Certainly, there are similarities between the two books. Both occupy the same spiritual landscape somewhere between Corfe and Cerne Abbas. Both are story cycles, though in the case of *The Chalk Giants* only three of the seven constituent stories—"Monkey and Pru and Sal", "The God House", and "The Beautiful One"—saw prior publication. Both open with a Dorset barmaid, Margaret or Martine, who then assumes the role of the multigirl in the subsequent stories. And both reflect the influence of Paul Nash.

But there are significant differences, also. *Pavane* begins in a radically transformed present and moves forward towards a more familiar world. *The Chalk Giants* begins in a familiar present and moves forward into a radically transformed world. The stories that constitute *Pavane* are linked more by allusion and symbolism than they are by the familiar continuities of plot or character. The stories that make up *The Chalk Giants*, on the other hand, are clearly intended to work as a unity, everything seen through the eyes of a single protagonist, Stan Potts. (This last may not have been apparent to readers of the first American edition of the book. The publisher insisted on removing the first two chapters, which introduced Potts, and the linking material between stories which situate them as Potts's dying visions, so that the book might be presented as a collection of disconnected stories.)

Nevertheless, the two books are linked. Roberts had the germ of *The Chalk Giants* when he was writing *Pavane*; they arose out of the same interests as much as out of the same landscape. Rather than the excessive loyalty, which Roberts saw as the recurrent theme in *Pavane*, he saw *The Chalk Giants* as "an extended study of sexual guilt ... [and] ... very much a 'black *Pavane*'" (Kincaid 1982: 10). In truth, *The Chalk Giants* is far more about Potts's unrequited sexual obsession with Martine than *Pavane* is about loyalty, but that isn't what really sets the two books in fruitful opposition to each other. For they are both shaped by the way belief emerges out of the landscape and in turn imposes a shape upon the landscape, and the damage that is done as religions grow more sophisticated and thus detach themselves from place. I think Roberts included *The Chalk Giants* among the works intended to rectify the perceived attack on Catholicism represented by *Pavane*. Yet the two works represent the same spiritual position, just approached from different perspectives. In *Pavane*, as we have seen, the old ways re-emerge from the land to support the growing opposition to the alien Church, the authority that owes nothing to the land. In *The Chalk Giants*, on the other hand, we see the nascent belief system being merged with the land, literally being carved upon it in the shape of the chalk figure, until at the end a new religion not linked to the soil arrives from outside and that will prompt the shedding of more blood. They are, thus, two sides of the same coin, and reading them in concert, each adds to the appreciation of the other.

The years that saw *Pavane* and *The Chalk Giants* were probably the height of Roberts's career. As well as these two story cycles, they saw what were perhaps his two finest short stories. "The Grain Kings" (1972), which again yoked character and landscape in a powerfully evocative way by once again drawing inspiration from Kipling, described life aboard giant harvesters in the vast grain fields of Alaska, combining implied climate change with sexual frustration and disillusionment that echoes *The*

Chalk Giants. Even more powerful was "Weinachtsabend" (1972). In a Britain that had surrendered to Nazi Germany even before the Second World War began, it tells of a Christmas holiday in the rural home of a Nazi functionary, and is full of small nuanced details that illuminate the menace and abuse of an imposed regime. Like both *Pavane* and *The Chalk Giants* it revolved around questions of what it was to be British, where loyalty lay, and the limits of obedience to a foreign autocracy.

These works continued to attract critical praise and a loyal readership, but he wouldn't quite regain the level of popularity that had greeted the original appearance of the *Pavane* stories. At its best, his prose remained as magical as ever; but by the mid- to late 1970s, critics were beginning to find that it wasn't always at its best. Some of the later stories were marred by what Dave Langford called "the feel of a middle-class Prospero" (Langford: 33), and M. John Harrison criticised the occasional laziness of his writing. At the same time as his sales began to decline during the late 1970s, so his ability to alienate his publishers also got in the way of his career. His last two short story collections from Gollancz, *Ladies from Hell* (1979) and *The Lordly Ones* (1986), never saw a paperback edition in the UK. And from 1986 onwards he was only ever published by small presses, by turns Kerosina, Morrigan, and Sirius, a couple of which at least were set up primarily to publish Keith Roberts, and he still managed to fall out with them. His last novel, *Drek Yarman* (2000), was only ever serialised in the first three issues of a short-lived British science fiction magazine, *Spectrum SF*, and has never seen volume publication. His succinct view of how he was regarded: "It's strange to watch oneself being written off in stages; like a sort of extended death in itself" (Letter to the author: 29 December 1994). None of this was helped by his failing health. In March 1990 he was diagnosed with multiple sclerosis; as a result, by 1994 he had had both legs amputated. His last years were spent in poverty and isolation. He died in October 2000.

And yet, if that all feels like a dying fall, perhaps even a case of career suicide, it is far from being the full story. During these years he continued to produce work of sometimes extraordinary quality. They were, in common with both *Pavane* and *The Chalk Giants*, stories in which the land, or the people, or both, were broken. *Molly Zero* tells of a typical adolescent female protagonist who escapes from an institution and sets out on a journey through a class-ridden, demoralised England that is physically broken up by fences and barriers. Her various encounters illustrate the process of social decay that led to this collapse. Another late work, *Kiteworld*, replicates the feel and structure of *Pavane* and *The Chalk Giants*, a story cycle that depicts a future land torn apart by religious division, with the eponymous kites guarding the borders against a nuclear threat so ancient that it is now little more than mythology. Linking the three story cycles, Nicholas Ruddick considered this "fascinating and provocative, far superior to most of what passes for contemporary science fiction" (Ruddick 1989a: 38). Two related stories, "The Lordly Ones" (1980) and "The Comfort Station" (1980), paint a picture of social collapse from the point of view of a slow-witted lavatory attendant, and display a level of empathy and sympathy rarely found in science fiction. And there was *Gráinne*, which would go on to win the BSFA Award for Best Novel and be shortlisted for the Arthur C. Clarke Award, part of a remarkable run of late career awards and nominations that rather belie any suggestion that he no longer had an audience. In this novel an avatar of Roberts himself becomes involved with a powerful, quasi-divine female figure who is initiating a new rebellion.

Discussing these late works, the *Science Fiction Encyclopedia* remarks: "In the sullen quietism that underlies the tales told, these books have little of the feel of sf" (Clute 2024). Which may suggest a reason why such an acclaimed author still seems to have dropped out of view. His interest in the ancient, the rural, the everyday, which meant that books like *Pavane* or *The Chalk Giants* could be read as historical fiction thinly disguised as science fiction, did not chime with the common perception of science fiction as concerned with the future, the urban, the extraordinary. His work went its own way and never attracted a school of writers following in his wake. And yet there is a thread that runs clearly from *Pavane* all the way through to his very last works: a fascination with the land, with belief, with dissent. In this short book I hope I have demonstrated how these consistent themes were all laid out in *Pavane*, how they were responsible for the particular richness and complexity of that extraordinary work, and consequently why *Pavane* remains an essential work in the history of science fiction.

Bibliography

Keith Roberts

A Heron Caught in Weeds. 1987. Salisbury: Kerosina Publications.

Drek Yarman. 2000. *Spectrum SF*, February–June 2000.
Gráinne. 1987. Salisbury: Kerosina Publications.
Kiteworld. 1985. London: Gollancz
Ladies from Hell. 1979. London: Gollancz.
Lemady: Episodes of a Writer's Life. 1997. Gillette, NJ: Wildside Press.
"Letter". 1975. *Foundation* 9 (November): 67–72.
Molly Zero. 1980. London: Gollancz.
Pavane. 1968 [1985]. London: Penguin.
"The Chalk Giant: Reflections by Keith Roberts". 1986. *Vector* 132 (June/July): 6–8.
The Chalk Giants. 1974. London: Hutchinson.
The Furies. 1966. London: Rupert Hart-Davis.
The Grain Kings. 1976. London: Hutchinson.
The Inner Wheel. 1970. London: Rupert Hart-Davis.
The Lordly Ones. 1986. London: Gollancz.
The Natural History of the P.H. 1988. Worcester Park: Kerosina Publications.

SECONDARY SOURCES

Butler, Andrew M. 2012. *Solar Flares: Science Fiction in the 1970s*. Liverpool: Liverpool University Press.
Cardinal, Roger. 1989. *The Landscape Vision of Paul Nash*. London: Reaktion.
Clute, John. 1995. *Look at the Evidence*. Liverpool: Liverpool University Press.
———. 2024. Keith Roberts. In *The Encyclopedia of Science Fiction*, 4th ed. https://sf-encyclopedia.com/entry/roberts_keith. Accessed 28 June 2024.
Fill, Sarah. 2016. Paul Nash, Surrealism and Prehistoric Dorset. In *Paul Nash*, ed. Emma Chambers, 49–57. London: Tate.
Hall, Graham. 1969. Pavane. *Speculation* 22 (April): 23–24.
Kincaid, Paul. 1982. Of Men and Machines: Keith Roberts Interviewed. *Vector* 108 (June): 6–12.
———. 1986. A Mosaic of Words. *Vector* 132 (June/July): 2–5.
———. 2014. Pavane. In *Call and Response*, 278–299. Harold Wood; Beccon Publications.
Langford, David. 2003. *Up Through an Empty House of Stars: Reviews and Essays 1980–2002*. Holicong, PA: Cosmos Books.
Platt, Charles. 1982. *Dream Makers: Volume II*. Strange Particle Press. Revised edition: 2021.
Priest, Christopher. 1968. Death of a Faery Queen. *Vector* 51 (October): 15–16, 21.
Ruddick, Nicholas. 1989a. Flaws in the Timestream: Unity and Disunity in Keith Roberts's Story-Cycles. *Foundation* 45 (Spring): 38–49.
———. 1989b. Flaws in the Timestream: Unity and Disunity in Keith Roberts's Story-Cycles: Part Two. *Foundation* 46 (Autumn): 14–26.

BIBLIOGRAPHY

WORKS BY KEITH ROBERTS

FICTION

Anita. 1970 [1976]. London: Millington. [Collection, includes: "The Witch", "Anita", "Outpatient", "The Simple for Love", "The Charm", "The Familiar", "The Jennifer", "The Middle Earth", "The War at Foxhanger", "Idiot's Lantern", "Timothy", "Cousin Ella Mae", "Sandpiper", "Junior Partner", "The Mayday"]

"Corfe Gate" (Original Version). 1966. *Impulse* Vol. 1, Issue 5: 7–68.

Drek Yarman. 2000. *Spectrum SF*, February–June 2000.

Gráinne. 1987. Salisbury: Kerosina Publications.

Kaeti & Company. 1986. Salisbury: Kerosina Publications. [Collection, includes: "Kaeti's Nights", "The Silence of the Land", "Kaeti and the Potman", "Kaeti and the Sky Person", "Kaeti and the Building", "Kaeti and the Tree", "Kaeti and the Hangman", "The Clocktower Girl", "Kaeti and the Zep", "The Dream Machine"]

Kaeti On Tour. 1992. Feltham: Sirius Book Company. [Collection, includes: "Kaeti and the Shadows", "The Tiger Sweater", "Kaeti and the Village", "Turndown", "Kaeti and the Airfield", "The Green Place", "The Aquatint", "The Bridge of Dreams", "Londinium"]

Kaetis Apocalypse. 1986. Salisbury: Kerosina Publications.

© The Author(s), under exclusive license to Springer Nature   77
Switzerland AG 2025
P. Kincaid, *Keith Roberts's* Pavane, Palgrave Science Fiction and
Fantasy: A New Canon,
https://doi.org/10.1007/978-3-031-71567-9

Kiteworld. 1985. London: Gollancz [Mosaic novel, includes: "Kitemaster", "Kitecadet", "Kitemistress", "Kitecaptain", "Kiteservant", "Kitewaif", "Kitemariner", "Kitekillers"]

Ladies from Hell. 1979. London: Gollancz. [Collection, includes: "Our Lady of Desperation", "The Shack at Great Cross Halt", "The Ministry of Children", "The Big Fans", "Missa Privata"]

Machines and Men. 1973. London: Hutchinson. [Collection, includes: "Manipulation", "Escapism", "Boulter's Canaries", "Sub-Lim", "Breakdown", "Therapy 2000", "The Deeps", "Manscarer", "Synth", "The Pace that Kills"]

Molly Zero. 1980. London: Gollancz.

Pavane. 1968 [1985]. London: Penguin. [Mosaic novel, includes: "Prologue", "The Lady Margaret", "The Signaller", "Brother John", "Lords and Ladies", "The White Boat", "Corfe Gate", "Coda"]

The Boat of Fate. 1971. London: Hutchinson.

The Chalk Giants. 1974. London: Hutchinson. [Mosaic novel, includes: "The Sun over a Low Hill", "Fragments", "Monkey and Pru and Sal", "The God House", "The Beautiful One", "Rand, Rat and the Dancing Man", "Usk the Jokeman"]

The Event. 1989. Scotforth, Lancs: Morrigan.

The Furies. 1966. London: Rupert Hart-Davis

The Grain Kings. 1976. London: Hutchinson. [Collection, includes: "Weihnachtsabend", "The White Boat", "The Passing of the Dragons", "The Trustie Tree", "The Lake of Tuonela", "The Grain Kings", "I Lose Medea"]

The Inner Wheel. 1970. London: Rupert Hart-Davis. [Mosaic novel, includes: "The Inner Wheel", "The Death of Libby Maynard", "The Everything Man"]

The Lordly Ones. 1986. London: Gollancz. [Collection, includes: "The Lordly Ones", "Ariadne Potts", "Sphairistike", "The Checkout", "The Comfort Station", "The Castle on the Hoop", "Diva"]

The Passing of the Dragons. 1977. New York; Berkley Books. [Collection, includes: "The Deeps", "Therapy 2000", "Boulter's Canaries", "Synth", "Manscarer", "Coranda", "The Grain Kings", "The White Boat", "The Passing of the Dragons", "The Lake of Tuonela", "I Lose Medea", "Weihnachtsabend"]

The Road to Paradise. 1988. Worcester Park: Kerosina Publications.

Winterwood and Other Hauntings. 1989. Scotforth, Lancs: Morrigan. [Collection, includes: "Susan", "The Scarlet Lady", "The Eastern Windows", "Winterwood", "Mrs Cibber", "The Snake Princess", "Everything in the Garden"]

Uncollected Stories

"Acclimatization" (as David Stringer) in *New Writings in SF 5*, 1965.

"Deterrent" (as Alistair Bevan) in *Science Fantasy 73*, June 1965.

"Equivalent for Giles" in *Tales from the Forbidden Planet* (ed Roz Kaveney) 1987.

"Flight of Fancy" in *Science Fantasy 69*, January 1965.

"High Eight" (as David Stringer) in *New Writings in SF 4*, 1965.
"Measured Perspective" in *Digital Dreams* (ed. David V. Barrett) 1990.
"Mrs Byres and the Dragon" in *Asimov's SF Magazine* August 1990.
"Piper's Wait" in *Other Edens* (ed. Christopher Evans & Robert Holdstock) 1987.
"Richenda" in *Magazine of Fantasy and Science* Fiction September 1985.
"Survey of the Third Planet" in *Magazine of Fantasy and Science Fiction*, January 1966.
"The Door" (as Alistair Bevan) in *Science Fantasy 74*, July 1965.
"The Flowers of the Valley" in *New Worlds 149*, April 1965.
"The Grey Wethers" in *Other Edens III* (ed Christopher Evans & Robert Holdstock) 1989.
"The Helmet-Maker's Wife" in *Ariel: The Book of Fantasy, Volume Two*, 1977.
"The Inn at the World's End" in *Heroic Visions* II, 1986.
"The Madman" (as Alistair Bevan) in *Science Fantasy 68*, December 1964.
"The Typewriter" (as Alistair Bevan) in *Science Fantasy 69*, January 1965.
"The Will of God" in *Asimov's SF Magazine* July 1991.
"The Worlds that Were" in *Science Fiction Monthly* vol 2, No 12, January 1976.
"The Wreck of the 'Kissing Bitch'" in *Warlocks and Warriors* (ed. Douglas Hill), 1971.
"Tremarest" in *Amazing Stories* November 1986.
"Unlikely Meeting" in *Interzone 88* October 1994.
"Virtual Reality" in *Spectrum 4* November 2000

NON-FICTION

A Heron Caught in Weeds. 1987. Salisbury: Kerosina Publications. [Poetry]
"Comment". 1996. *St. James Guide to Science Fiction Writers: Fourth Edition.* Edited by Jay P. Pederson, 780. New York; St James Press.
"Introduction". 1983. *British Science Fiction Writers: Keith Roberts.* Edited by Paul Kincaid and Geoff Rippington. Folkestone: British Science Fiction Association, 5–6.
Irish Encounters. 1988. Worcester Park: Kerosina Publications.
Lemady: Episodes of a Writer's Life. 1997. Gillette, NJ: Wildside Press.
"Letter". 1975. *Foundation* 9 (November): 67–72.
"The Chalk Giant: Reflections by Keith Roberts". 1986. *Vector* 132 (June/July): 6–8.
The Natural History of the P.H. 1988. Worcester Park: Kerosina Publications.

SECONDARY SOURCES

Aldiss, Brian with David Wingrove. 1986 [1988]. *Trillion Year Spree*. London: Paladin.

Allan, Nina. 2018. The Fourfold Library (8): Keith Roberts, *Pavane*. *Foundation* 131: 69–71.

Barron, Neil, ed. 2004. *Anatomy of Wonder: A Critical Guide to Science Fiction*. 5th ed. Westport, CT: Libraries Unlimited.

Bilson, Fred. 2005. The Colonialist's Fear of Colonisation and the Alternate Worlds of Ward Moore, Philip K. Dick and Keith Roberts. *Foundation* 94 (Summer): 50–63.

Bonfiglioli, Kyril. 1966. Editorial. *Impulse* Vol. 1, Issue 5: 2–3, 79.

Bould, Mark, and Michelle Reid, eds. 2005. *Parietal Games: Critical Writings by and on M. John Harrison*. London: Science Fiction Foundation. Foundation Studies in Science Fiction 5.

Budrys, Algis. 1985. *Benchmarks: Galaxy Bookshelf*. Carbondale: Southern Illinois University Press.

———. 2012. *Benchmarks Continued: F&SF 'Books' Columns 1975–1982*. Reading: Ansible Editions.

Burgess, Anthony. 1984. *Ninety-Nine Novels: The Best in English since 1939*. London: Allison & Busby.

Butler, Andrew M. 2012. *Solar Flares: Science Fiction in the 1970s*. Liverpool: Liverpool University Press.

Cardinal, Roger. 1989. *The Landscape Vision of Paul Nash*. London: Reaktion.

Clarke, Jim. 2019. *Science Fiction and Catholicism: The Rise and Fall of the Robot Papacy*. Canterbury: Gylphi.

Clute, John. 1979. Keith Roberts. In *The Encyclopedia of Science Fiction*, 1st ed., 499–500. London: Granada.

———. 1995. *Look at the Evidence*. Liverpool: Liverpool University Press.

———. 2024. Keith Roberts. In *The Encyclopedia of Science Fiction*, 4th ed. https://sf-encyclopedia.com/entry/roberts_keith. Accessed 28 June 2024.

Davidson, H.R. Ellis. 1964 [1975]. *Gods and Myths of Northern Europe*. Harmondsworth: Penguin.

Fill, Sarah. 2016. Paul Nash, Surrealism and Prehistoric Dorset. In *Paul Nash*, ed. Emma Chambers, 49–57. London: Tate.

Gillespie, Bruce. 1994. The Not-Quite Career of Keith Roberts. *Scratch Pad* 14 (December): 1–7.

Goddard, Jim. 2000. Keith Roberts: A Remembrance. *Locus* 478 (November): 68.

Hall, Graham. 1969. Pavane. *Speculation* 22 (April): 23–24.

Hanna, Judith. 1985. Second Glance. *Vector* 126 (June/July): 11.

Hazard, Paul. 1935 [2013]. *The Crisis of the European Mind 1680–1715*. Trans. J. Lewis May. New York: New York Review Books.

Hurst, L.J. 1985. A Timeless Dance: Keith Roberts' *Pavane* Re-examined. *Vector* 124/125 (April–May): 17–19.

Hutchinson, Dave. 2016. Science Fiction in Your Own Back Yard: *Pavane* by Keith Roberts. *Reactor*. https://reactormag.com/science-fiction-in-your-own-back-yard-pavane-by-keith-roberts/. Accessed 15 April 2024.

Jordan, Michael. 1992 [1995]. *The Encyclopedia of Gods*. London: Kyle Cathie.

Kaveney, Roz. 1981. Science Fiction in the 1970s: Some Dominant Themes and Personalities. *Foundation* 22 (June): 5–35.

Kincaid, Paul. 1982. Of Men and Machines: Keith Roberts Interviewed. *Vector* 108 (June): 6–12.

———. 1986. A Mosaic of Words. *Vector* 132 (June/July): 2–5.

———. 1996. Roberts, Keith. In *St. James Guide to Science Fiction Writers: Fourth Edition*, ed. Jay P. Pederson, 780–781. New York: St James Press.

———. 2001. Future Historical: The Fiction of Keith Roberts. *Steam Engine Time* 3 (December): 20–24.

———. 2005. Landscape in the Fiction of Keith Roberts. *Foundation* 93 (Spring): 9–66.

———. 2008. The Furies. In *What It Is We Do When We Read Science Fiction*, 173–187. Harold Wood: Beccon Publications.

———. 2014. Pavane. In *Call and Response*, 278–299. Harold Wood: Beccon Publications.

Kipling, Rudyard. 1906 [1975]. *Puck of Pook's Hill*. London: Piccolo.

Langford, David. 2003. *Up Through an Empty House of Stars: Reviews and Essays 1980–2002*. Holigong, PA: Cosmos Books.

Luckhurst, Roger. 2005. *Science Fiction*. Cambridge: Polity Press.

MacCulloch, Diarmaid. 2003. *Reformation: Europe's House Divided, 1490–1700*. London: Allen Lane.

Matless, David. 2016 [2019]. *Landscape and Englishness*. Second Expanded Edition. London: Reaktion Books.

Peek, Bernie. 1986. Exercises in Landscape. *Vector* 132 (June/July): 12–13.

Platt, Charles. 1982. *Dream Makers: Volume II*. Strange Particle Press. Revised edition: 2021.

Priest, Christopher. 1965. New Wave—Prozines. *Zenith Speculation* 8 (March): 9–11.

———. 1968. Death of a Faery Queen. *Vector* 51 (October): 15–16, 21.

Pringle, David. 1985. *Science Fiction the 100 Best Novels: An English-Language Selection, 1949–1984*. London: Xanadu.

Rowan, Iain. 2001. Pavane. *Infinity Plus*. http://www.infinityplus.co.uk/nonfiction/pavane.htm. Accessed 15 April 2024.

Ruddick, Nicholas. 1989a. Flaws in the Timestream: Unity and Disunity in Keith Roberts's Story-Cycles. *Foundation* 45 (Spring): 38–49.

————. 1989b. Flaws in the Timestream: Unity and Disunity in Keith Roberts's Story-Cycles: Part Two. *Foundation* 46 (Autumn): 14–26.

————. 1990. Flaws in the Timestream: Unity and Disunity in Keith Roberts's Story-Cycles (Conclusion). *Foundation* 47 (Winter): 33–42.

Suvin, Darko. 1983. Victorian Science Fiction, 1871–85: The Rise of the Alternative History Sub-Genre. *Science Fiction Studies* 10 (Part 2): 148–169.

Tawney, R.H. 1926. *Religion and the Rise of Capitalism.* London: Pelican. 1937 edition.

Tew, Steven. 1985. Second Glance. *Vector* 126 (June/July): 10–11.

INDEX

© The Author(s), under exclusive license to Springer Nature   83
Switzerland AG 2025
P. Kincaid, *Keith Roberts's* Pavane, Palgrave Science Fiction and
Fantasy: A New Canon,
https://doi.org/10.1007/978-3-031-71567-9

GPSR Compliance

The European Union's (EU) General Product Safety Regulation (GPSR) is a set of rules that requires consumer products to be safe and our obligations to ensure this.

If you have any concerns about our products, you can contact us on ProductSafety@springernature.com

In case Publisher is established outside the EU, the EU authorized representative is:

Springer Nature Customer Service Center GmbH
Europaplatz 3
69115 Heidelberg, Germany

The manufacturer's authorised representative in the EU is Springer
Nature Customer Service Centre GmbH, Europaplatz 3, 69115 Heidelberg,
Germany. If you have any concerns regarding our products, please
contact ProductSafety@springernature.com

Printed and bound by CPI Group (UK) Ltd, Croydon, CR0 4YY
27/04/2026
02097563-0011